BRING IT ON

by Jenny Markas

**Based on the motion picture screenplay
written by Jessica Bendinger**

SCHOLASTIC INC.

New York   Toronto   London   Auckland   Sydney
Mexico City   New Delhi   Hong Kong

ISBN 0-439-19454-7

Designed by Louise Bova

12 11 10 9 8 7 6 5 4 3 2 1   0 1 2 3 4 5 6/0

Printed in the U.S.A.
First Scholastic printing, September 2000

CHAPTER 1

You don't know. You *can't* know. Unless you're like me, and you've been cheering since you were six and so totally proud of yourself in your red-and-white Tiny Tots uniform.

To you, the words "pep rally" probably don't mean much. Oh, maybe a good time, rockin' the gym and stomping the bleachers while you watch some girls jump around and yell. Or maybe you're the type who thinks it's all bull, that school spirit is for weenies.

Me? Mention the words "pep rally" and my pulse starts to pound. My breath comes a little quicker, I stand up straighter, my mouth automatically starts smiling, and I bet my eyes get really bright.

Why? 'Cause I'm a cheerleader.

And this is how it looks from *my* perspective.

The gym is practically shaking as the music booms up through the rafters. The bleachers are packed and everybody's psyched, ready to see us nail another outrageous routine.

A huge banner hung from the rafters waves slowly above us: RANCHO CARNE TOROS!

We echo that.

> "We are the Toros!
> The mighty, mighty Toros!
> We're so Titanic,
> We must be Toros!"

We're moving, we're grooving, we're all out, dancing and strutting our stuff. Everybody yells in unison:

> "I'm sexy, I'm cute.
> I'm popular to boot.
> I'm major, great hair.
> The boys all like to stare.
> I'm wanted. I'm hot.
> I'm everything you're not.
> I'm pretty. I'm cool.
> I dominate the school.
> I'm rockin'. I smile.
> And many think I'm vile!
> Hate us 'cause we're beautiful?
> Well, we don't like you either!
> We're cheerleaders.
> We are cheerleaders!"

Then we start our tumbling runs. Big Red, naturally, goes first. She's captain. She throws a couple of flips then stands, hands on hips. Her coppery ringlets tumble all over her shoulders. "Call me Big Red!"

Next is an Asian girl with a tan the color of mahogany, courtesy of Hawaiian Sunbeds. "I'm Wu-Wu-Whitney!" she hollers.

A blonde is next. She looks like the girl in that shampoo ad, the one who nearly dies with pleasure as she's tossing her silky locks all over the place. "Cu-Cu-Cu-Courtney!"

Behind her cartwheels a girl with so much attitude it sends a frosty blast across the gym. Her jet-black bob springs perfectly into place the second she stands still. "Dude, it's Da-Darcy!"

"I'm big, bad Carver!" cries the girl who lands next. So she is. Carver isn't your delicate, malnourished type. That girl has some meat on her bones. And she can *fly*.

Next to her, Kasey looks scrawny. And her braces could blind you. "Just call me Kasey!"

Then Big Red jumps into center stage again. "I'm still Big Red!" she yells. The rest of the squad freezes, then turns to point at her. Big Red gets *down*. She's busting moves nobody's ever seen before. The crowd starts to go wild.

> "I sizzle, I scorch.
> But now I pass the torch.
> The ballots are in,
>   and one girl had to win.

She's perky, she's fun,
    and now she's number one.
K-k-kick it, Torrance!
Tu-tu-tu-Torrance!"

That's my cue. I run into the center of the
semicircle on the floor. My smile is huge.

"I'm strong and I'm loud!
I'm gonna make you proud!
I'm Tu-tu-Torrance!
Your new captain, Torrance!
LET'S GO, TOROS!"

We blast into the final segment of our routine,
synchronized down to the last nanosecond. Then
it's time for our big jump, a toe-touch. I smile
wider. Wider.

And then, as I go into liftoff, I touch my hand
to my head. I feel a strange sensation. A lumpy,
plastic sensation.

I've forgotten to take the curlers out of my
hair.

My head is completely covered in huge pink
rollers.

I look like an idiot.

And everyone's noticed.

the organization. Today is the orientation. Don't forget to

I was in the cafeteria following the last

CHAPTER 2

"**A**AAAHHHHH!!!!" The alarm went off and I sat bolt upright in my bed, screaming. Not that dream again. It's so, like, *predictable*. A cheerleader's worst nightmare.

Though I had to admit I did like the part about Big Red naming me the new captain.

Somebody had to get the job. Big Red was heading off to college, and the squad needed new leadership. I was itching to take over. Being squad captain in my senior year would be the pinnacle of my high school cheering career. I knew I was the natural choice, but Big Red was unpredictable. She was capable of anything. She might even name that airhead Kasey captain!

I mused about the situation as I went about my morning routine. Beating my twelve-year-old brother, Justin, into the bathroom, I totally aroma-therapized myself by showering with energizing bath gel. I did my makeup in the usual 7.5 minutes and threw on the outfit I'd laid out the night before. (Okay, so I'm organized. Don't hate me.)

I was in the kitchen, downing my power smoothie, when I heard Aaron's horn outside. I felt my stomach do a little flip. This was it! My boyfriend was driving me to school for the last time. He was on his way to college. We weren't breaking up or anything, but things were bound to change. It was, like, inevitable.

My parents, Mr. and Mrs. Shipman, Esquires (they're both attorneys), were lugging boxes of files out to their Escort Wagon (could we *have* a lamer car?).

"Hey, Mr. and Mrs. S.!" called Aaron, from the driver's seat of his Geo Tracker. "Guess what? I'm goin' to college!"

Aaron looked, as usual, awesome. Tan, buff to the max, and not a hair out of place. Until he graduated he'd been on our cheerleading squad (yup, it's co-ed), and every girl in the school had wanted him.

My parents, to put it mildly, weren't impressed by Aaron.

"Oh, look," said my dad, in this sarcastic tone. "It's Aaron. And he's going to college."

Aaron's vehicle was loaded with . . . guy stuff. A stereo, a mini-fridge, a microwave, a pair of skis, about six overstuffed duffel bags.

"Hello, Aaron," said my mother, trying to be civil. "Congratulations."

"Thanks!" beamed Aaron. "Can I help you guys with those boxes?"

"No! I mean, we're fine, really. Stay in your vehicle." My mom looked alarmed.

I bounded out of the house, kissing my dad on the cheek as I headed for the passenger seat of the Geo. "Bye! Be back later!"

"Bye!" chorused the 'rents.

Aaron grinned at me as I jumped in. I could just picture Mom and Dad exchanging a look and shaking their heads. They just don't get Aaron.

"Hey," I said. I leaned over to kiss him.

He pulled back. "C'mon, Tor. Not in front of your parents."

Aaron can be so . . . I don't know. I shook my head. Then I glanced around at all the stuff in the back. "So, are you excited?"

"I'm totally stoked," he said. "I mean, it's college! It's just . . . you know, I'm gonna miss you."

"Really?"

"Of course. But next year, it'll be you and me, reunited at Cal State Dominguez Hills!" He grinned again. "I'll be the experienced sophomore, and you'll be the hot new freshman."

I tried to smile.

Aaron hit the horn as we turned into the school parking lot. My smile broadened as I checked out the marquee sign out in front: HOME OF THE RANCHO CARNE TOROS, it proclaimed, FIVE-TIME NATIONAL CHEERLEADING CHAMPIONS.

Oh, yeah.

Did I forget to mention that? Our squad isn't just any old pom-pom-shaking bunch of high-kickers. We rule.

Aaron looked over and saw my smile. "Remember to act surprised when you get captain, okay?"

"Don't jinx me!" I smacked him.

He pulled into his old spot. The rest of the squad was arriving for practice. All the girls from my dream, plus Jan and Leslie, the guys who put the "co" in co-ed.

Whitney and Courtney ran right up to Aaron's window. They were practically drooling. "Hey, Aaron," said Courtney, giving him her best smile, "good luck at school."

"Aaron!" whined Whitney. "Come to one last practice! We're lost without you!"

Aaron shook his head. "Sorry, guys. Gotta run. Goin' to college!"

"You're not staying for the vote?" I asked, disappointed.

"I really gotta beat traffic. Don't want to be late for my first day." Before I could say anything, he leaned over and kissed me on the lips. He *really* kissed me. I guess he figured it was going to have to last us a while. "Trust me," he whispered. "You're gonna get it." He smiled his sexiest smile.

I did my best to smile back. Then I grabbed my gear and hopped out. "Bye!" I called softly.

He blew me a kiss, then peeled out. As I watched the Tracker disappear into the distance, Kasey walked by.

"You're so lucky, Torrance," she said.

"Yeah . . ." I said. Sometimes I wasn't so sure.

Leslie joined me as Kasey bopped off. He made a face. "Just 'cause all those idiots worship Aaron doesn't mean you have to stay with him, you know?"

I knew he meant well. Still. "Haven't you ever heard of a little thing called loyalty?"

"Honey, you put the 'oy' in loyalty."

"Nice splice." I held out my hand and he smacked it. Leslie's okay.

But did he vote for me? I wondered as I left him, heading toward the locker room.

The place was buzzing. There were enough ankle braces, wrist guards, and lower back belts to open a medical supply store (cheerleading may look like fun, but it definitely takes its toll on the human body).

"Did you vote?" I heard Whitney ask Courtney.

"Yeah," Courtney answered. She was taping her ribs. "Darcy thinks she should get captain because her dad pays for everything."

Whitney snorted. "He should use some of that money to buy her a clue."

Over in the next row of lockers, Kasey was taping Darcy's ankle. "Courtney'll get captain. The guys love her."

"But she is so not worthy," Darcy said, examining her nails.

Just then, Big Red appeared, holding a list. Everybody snapped to attention. "Yo! Do I have all your votes?"

A couple of girls handed slips of paper to Big Red, and she left the locker room.

I'd never been overly fond of Big Red, but watching her leave the room just then made me think of something. "You know," I said, "we should have gotten Big Red a gift. Or at least someone should say something."

Courtney and Whitney looked at each other. I could just imagine what they were thinking. "Pass," said Courtney, resisting — just barely — the impulse to dis Big Red.

"Good riddance," agreed Whitney. "She's history. Why bother brownnosing?"

"I am not brownnosing!" I glared at Whitney. "She's the departing captain. It's, like, a hallowed tradition." They stared at me. "Come on," I went on. "You know she helped make this team what it is."

"No one will miss Big Red, Tor," said Whitney.

"It's her last practice!" I protested. "And she did lead us to the fifth of five successive national championships. How would you feel?"

Courtney snickered. "Big Red *has* no feelings."

Hmm. Courtney could have a point there.

"Let's do this, children!" Big Red reappeared, clapping her hands. "Outside! Now! Your lack of speed disgusts me."

Courtney brushed by me. "You were so right, Tor," she said sarcastically. "Flowers *would* have been nice."

"Or a cake," added Whitney.

I followed them out onto the football field. The squad spread out and everybody started doing their warm-up stretches. Big Red stood on the bleachers, watching us.

"Big Dread," whispered Whitney as she did a hamstring stretch. "They'll have to rip the torch out of her hands."

"Her reign of terror is over," Courtney whispered back.

Those two never give it up.

"No more ten-mile runs," said Whitney, lunging into a runner's stretch.

"Still," Whitney added, doing the drama-queen thing, "there were good times . . ."

Courtney cracked up.

I wanted to, but I was too nervous. The moment of truth was approaching. Fast. Any minute now, Big Red was going to announce her successor.

Big Red cleared her throat.

We all stopped stretching.

"You guys are all great athletes, thanks in large part to me," she began, with typical Big Red humility. "I know your new captain will keep the tradition alive — leading you to the sixth National Cheerleading Championship you know is yours."

Yada, yada, yada. When was she going to get to the point?

"So, meet your new leader," she went on. "Torrance Shipman."

Everybody whooped, except for Courtney and Whitney, who rolled their eyes at each other.

"No way!" I said. This was what I'd been hoping for, planning for, maybe even expecting. But somehow, it was so . . . unexpected. "I can't believe it, you guys!" I looked around. "Awesome." Everybody crowded around me, holding up hands for high fives.

Up in the bleachers, Big Red was nodding. *This is good,* I thought. *Yes. This is good.*

CHAPTER 3

"**O**kay, listen up!" Big Red was gone and the squad was mine, all mine. I felt a surge of power. Was this how it felt to command an army? I could tell them to do anything, and they'd have to do it. After all, I was captain.

We had the football field to ourselves. We were stretched and toned and ready to work out. I had a sudden urge that I couldn't deny. Why not go for it? "I know it's early in the season," I told the squad — *my* squad — "but I'd like to try a ground-up wolf's wall."

Silence.

Just for a second. Then Carver spoke up. "Excellent," she said. "God, Torrance, you are, like, so bold and beautiful. A wolf's wall."

She was serious, but the rest of the squad cracked up. Darcy was laughing so hard she could hardly stay on her feet.

Courtney walked over to me and put her hand on my forehead. "Torrance has got the fever, people," she reported.

"What's a wolf's wall?" Kasey was probably the only one clueless enough to have to ask.

Leslie smiled and did a back flip. "Only the hardest pyramid known to cheerleading," he said when he'd landed. "And mankind."

Darcy quit laughing long enough to add, "The words 'big' and 'britches' come to mind."

"She's crazy!" Whitney raved. "She'll kill us all!"

"Hello?" Courtney said to me. "Some of us have not spent the whole summer working out." She glanced at Carver. "Or ever . . ."

"Come on!" I put my hands on my hips. Had I just been named captain of the wimps? How much fun was *that* going to be? "Let's be different for once. We can't just rest on our laurels. Where's your drive?"

"In my car," Jan cracked. "And why does everybody always say that about laurels? Maybe a laurel is a good place to rest."

"Let's graduate in one piece, shall we?" asked Darcy. "I mean, this is the first practice of the year. The wolf's wall is awfully emulous."

Silence. Bewildered looks.

"It's an SAT word," she explained. "It means 'ambitious.'"

I looked around and noticed something. They might be joking around, but the fact was they were scared. Just plain scared.

Then it happened. Leslie spoke up. "Let's do

this," he said. He jumped to my side. I saw the others exchange glances. They were coming around. I just knew it.

"Can I fly?" Carver asked. That girl just loved to leap through the air.

"Sure," I agreed. The rest of the squad grumbled, but that did it. They got to their feet. We started to build the wall.

This squad has been working together so long that I hardly had to say a thing. The bases took up their positions. Then the mounters. Then Carver began to climb up their backs.

The pyramid crumbled.

"Come on," I said. We started over.

It went down again. A heap of tangled bodies lay on the ground. I heard moans. "Again," I insisted.

It took four tries altogether. But finally, Carver was crouching up there at the tippy-top, three body-lengths high. Higher than any Toros cheerleader had gone before.

"Carver, can you full out?" I asked, looking for the final extension.

"You bet I can!" she yelled. "Thanks for letting me fly, you guys!" She went for it. But she must have been off balance when she tried to straighten up. With a bloodcurdling scream, she fell through the air and landed with a thud.

Oops.

CHAPTER 4

Okay, so maybe my first stab at leadership wasn't a total success. I do have to say that the ambulance got there amazingly fast.

That night in my room, I worked the phone for a while. "Traction?" I shrieked, when I had Carver's doctor on the line. I looked around at the plaques, ribbons, and trophies that cover every wall and shelf in my room. My decorating scheme is, like, Early Cheerleader. "But she's definitely not gonna die, right? Okay. Six weeks in the hospital? But that's unacceptable. Regionals are in a month!"

I paused to listen as the doctor babbled on. "Yes," I finally agreed. "I realize that the human healing mechanism does not care about cheerleading. But I do!" I hung up.

How were we going to make it through regionals without our flyer? Stunts just don't cut it if there's nobody to throw around. I made a mental note to put in a call to Carver later that evening, then I grumpily headed down to the kitchen.

"Hi, honey," said my mom. She was going over some paperwork. Justin was sitting next to her, plowing through a bowl of chocolate ice cream. "How was your day?"

"I got captain," I reported.

"And you sent a girl to the hospital on your first day!" remarked Justin-the-clever. "Aye-aye, cap'n!" He snapped a cheery salute.

"You were listening on the phone!" I turned to Mom. "Mom!"

She shot Justin a look.

"It's true," admitted Justin. "She really ought to have a private line, you know. She's growing up so fast." He made puppy-dog eyes.

"Justin, go away," said my mom. He left. Then Mom picked up an envelope and pulled out an official-looking paper. Gulp. It was my class schedule.

"This blistering academic schedule shouldn't get in your way," said Mom sarcastically, waving it at me. "You must be very happy."

I sighed. "Why can't you just accept the fact that I'm not a genius?" I asked. "It just kills you that I'm not an honor student." Make no mistake, I'm no dumb blonde. But I'm not exactly in touch with my inner Einstein, either.

"What kills me is that you barely make time to study. If you studied as much as you cheer, you'd be getting great grades. Your priorities are —"

I didn't let her finish. "Those are *your* priorities. Mine are just fine for me." My parents just don't get the cheering thing. Never have, never will.

"Look, you can cheer all you want," Mom said.

What was this, reverse psychology? I narrowed my eyes.

"All I'm saying," she continued, "is that college might be less of a shock if you take an extra lab or language course or something. What do you think?"

I pondered. It was time to cut a deal. "Will advanced chem get you off my back?"

"Not completely. But it'll help."

"Done." I got up to go. Then I turned around. "You know, mothers have killed to get their daughters on squads," I said, remembering that news story a while back.

"That mother didn't kill anyone. She hired a hit man. Big difference."

I glared at her.

"It is only cheerleading, honey," she said gently. Then she smiled. "I mean, Captain Honey."

Ouch. *Only* cheerleading. How many times had I heard *that* in my life? "You know, a normal parent would've just said, 'Congratulations.'" I stomped off to my room, slammed the door, and settled in for a long sulk, with only the comfort of my stuffed animals.

CHAPTER 5

"**I**t's only the second day of school," I said to Leslie and Jan. "Can you believe Darcy?"

We were sitting on the front steps, a spot we *own*, waiting for the first bell.

"She's all out on that SAT thing," Leslie agreed, shaking his head.

Darcy and Kasey walked toward us. "Hit me," said Kasey.

Darcy clapped out a rhythm, chanting her vocabulary words and gesturing dramatically for emphasis. "*Turgid*: I'm bloated but I'm *tensile*, withstanding stress and *tantamount's* equivalent while *paramount* is dominant! *Quotidian* is daily, don't get *querulous* complaining, try *quiescence*, that's stillness, be a *sybarite*, a pleasure seeker, *recondite*, few know it, I'm *vociferous*: loud, vocal, but not *wizened*, that's wrinkled, we'll end on *tenesmus!*"

Leslie and I whooped and applauded. Darcy was *on*.

Kasey wrinkled her brow. "What's *tenesmus*?" she asked.

I raised my hand.

"Torrance?" Darcy called on me.

"The unsuccessful straining associated with the urgent need to number-one or number-two," I reported. I've been studying, too. Darcy and I tagged up.

"Ew!" Kasey made a face. "There's a word for that? SAT's are beyond vile."

She and Darcy headed on into the school.

As they disappeared inside, two football players sauntered by. They're so muscle-bound they can barely walk. Idiots.

"Whoo," yodeled one of them, spotting Jan and Leslie. "It's sexy Leslie and Jan, Jan, the cheerleading man."

"Hey, ladies," added the other guy, who thinks he's hot just 'cause he's a quarterback.

Jan stood up, fists clenched. He gets so tired of that routine. Les grabbed his shirt, holding him back. "Just because we've won more trophies than you guys is no reason to get all malignant," he told the football players.

Leslie shook his head. "Let it go. They've never even won a single game. It's gotta be pretty tough on them." He paused. "Also, they're total morons," he added.

"No lie," I said. "Hey, Les, you better tell me you're in advanced chem first period."

"Advanced chem, first period," he said agreeably.

"If you already have a lab partner, I'm dead."

"Torrance." He looked impatient. "It's only the second day of school and already your academic insecurity bit is completely tired."

"Said the straight-A student to the queen of the B minus," I muttered. He just doesn't understand.

"So," Leslie changed the subject, "you know, everybody's saying your ambition broke Carver's leg."

"Huh," I said thoughtfully. "When actually it was the angle at which she slammed into the ground."

"Kasey sent out a massive e-mail last night." Leslie laughed. "She misspelled 'leg.'"

"Get out!"

He nodded. "Two g's. Apparently, Carver gets home-schooling for the next three months."

Old news. "I talked to her last night. Amazing that a girl in traction could be so upbeat. Replacing her is going to be a nightmare."

"That's why you're the captain, captain," said Leslie, just as the first bell rang.

CHAPTER 6

Whoa. Major babe alert.

I was staring at the guy in front of the room.

So was everybody else.

Study hall, last period. It had been a long day. Advanced chem was only the beginning. I was so ready to be out of there.

But then *he* glided in. Dressed in vintage creepers, low-slung jeans, and a black T-shirt, old, but well preserved, that said *The Clash*.

Ignoring our stares, he handed a note to the monitor. The monitor read it, then looked up.

"Everyone," he said, "we have a new student transferring from Mission Hills High in Los Angeles. Please welcome Cliff . . ." He stumbled over his last name. "Pantone?" he asked, pronouncing the second syllable like the number one.

"Pantone," said the new guy quickly, pronouncing it like "dial tone."

Not quickly enough. Everybody was already cracking up. It's never easy being new.

Cliff (love that name) just smiled an "I can take it" smile and waited for the giggles to subside.

The monitor pointed to a seat in the back.

Right next to me.

Cliff caught my eye, noticed I wasn't partaking in the laughfest, and raised an eyebrow. He took a step toward me.

Just then, one of the idiot football players — I think he's a tight end — faked a sneeze. "Loser!"

Cliff shook his head.

A bunch of other players (they always cluster, like ants) snickered.

Cliff rolled his eyes and kept walking.

"Loser!" Another "sneeze."

Cliff stopped in his tracks. "Are you kidding me?"

The football players looked confused.

This was getting interesting.

"Was that the 'loser sneeze'? In this day and age?" Cliff sounded incredulous. "That's so 1900s. Nobody does that anymore." He stopped to consider. "I don't think," he added. "Wait, lemme see. When I lived in Detroit, did they do the 'loser sneeze'?" He shook his head. "No, they hit people a lot . . . there was fighting . . ."

The tight end was looking bewildered. I was all ears.

"What about L.A.? Mmm, lotta attitude, but no 'loser sneeze.'" He held up his hands in mock despair. "No, I'm pretty sure the 'loser sneeze' is officially dead. Sorry." He gave the tight end a bright smile and turned away.

The guy had no idea what to do. "Loser," he sneezed again. The other players cracked up.

"Nice," said one of them.

"Dude," said another to the tight end, "you must be allergic to losers!" They tagged up. This witticism made them all practically hysterical.

Cliff just shook his head and started walking again, straight to the desk next to mine.

"I don't think they got the memo about the 'loser sneeze,'" I said.

Cliff shrugged. "Doesn't seem like it."

Neither of us spoke for a moment — but I could swear there was something buzzing between us, like, in the atmosphere.

He met my eyes. "Cliff," he said, introducing himself.

"Torrance. So, how's the first day shaping up?" I forced myself to sound casual, even though it seemed as if every word *mattered*. I didn't know why, exactly, but I wanted — really wanted — this guy to like me.

"Nicely," he answered. "Thanks." He reached over to check the cover of the textbook I was reading. "Yikes! Advanced chem?"

Ha! He was impressed. "Afraid so. Intimidated?"

He grinned. "A little."

"Really?" I wasn't sure I liked that answer.

"No, not really." He smiled at me, a nice, open smile. I couldn't help smiling back. Advanced chemistry, indeed. There was definitely *some* kind of chemistry happening here.

I motioned toward his T-shirt. "Is that your band or something?" I asked.

"The Clash?" asked Cliff, after a quick look down to check. "Uh, no. British punk band, circa 1977 to 1983ish. Original lineup, anyway."

Guys can be so cute when they start talking about their interests. "How vintage," I commented.

Just then, the bell rang. Oooh, bad timing. I had the feeling, from the way he was looking at me, that Cliff might just be on the verge of asking me out.

On the other hand, what was I thinking? Aaron had left a mere forty-eight hours earlier. Had I forgotten him already?

Cliff looked bummed when I stood up and started to pull my stuff together. "So, I'll see you around?" he asked.

"Looks like it," I said with a smile. I turned and headed out of the room, with the distinct sensation that he was following me with his eyes.

CHAPTER 7

Cliff was still on my mind when I met with the rest of the squad in the gym. We were holding tryouts to replace Carver.

A line of kids waited outside the gym nervously. Inside, the squad and I did a quick huddle.

"Bring on the tyros, the neophytes, and the dilletanti!" announced Darcy.

"Enough with the SAT words." Jan rolled his eyes.

Darcy ignored him. "Are we sure Carver's not malingering?" she asked.

I nodded. "And she's cool with this. I talked to her. We have to get the new person up to speed for regionals." That was only four weeks away.

"Do we really have to go through this tryout masquerade?" asked Courtney. "Let's just forget it and pick somebody. Whitney's little sister Jamie is perfect. She's tiny and she'll be easy to toss."

"If she's the best, Jamie's got it," I said. "But we have to see everyone."

Whitney moaned. "That'll take forever. Besides, me and Jamie tan the *exact* same shade. Consider the visuals."

"No cheating. No nepotism." I was firm. "We see everyone."

"You put the *tor* in torture, Torrance," Courtney cracked.

"Nice splice," Whitney whispered.

I just rolled my eyes. "Point taken. Now, go open the moat, princess," I directed, pointing toward the doors of the gym.

The first girl was massively nervous. She kept starting over as she tried to get through her cheer. "Okay, wait," she'd say, stopping in mid-yell. "That was horrible. Let me start over." Then she'd go for three seconds and stop again. "No, no, wait! I got it. Okay —"

Next!

We saw them all, just like I had said we would. And believe me, it was no picnic. We sat through the girl who thought she was all that but was so hunting, the girl who seemed angry at the world, and the guy who looked like he belonged in a tutu, dancing *Swan Lake*. Another girl had just broken up with her boyfriend; she cried through her whole routine.

Next.

An awkward kid with glasses and braces showed off his best "robot."

Next.

Jamie was up. "Here's our girl," Whitney said.

Jamie was *tiny*. And I had to admit she wasn't bad. She wasn't great, but she wasn't bad. She moved through her routine looking bored, and finished with a slightly off-balance jump. Then she winked at us, like, "I know it's in the bag," and ran off.

"Nice tan," I commented to Whitney and Courtney. What else was there to say about her?

Next up was a guy who started belting out a Broadway song. Great singer. Wrong audition. "The tryouts for *Pippin* are in the auditorium," I informed him.

"That's it, isn't it?" I checked the list. We were done. It looked like Jamie was our best bet after all.

Then the door opened one last time. "Or, maybe not," I noted. Was this another Toros wanna-be? She sure didn't look the part. She was a brunette, maybe sixteen or so. She had on low-slung cholo trousers topped with a sleeveless undershirt. Her bra straps — Day-Glo, no less — hung out for all to see. And she had a bold, black tribal tattoo around one bicep.

"Whoa," Jan whispered under his breath.

"Excuse me," Whitney whispered to Courtney, "where'd she park her Harley?"

Courtney giggled. Then she turned to the girl. "Tattoos are strictly verboten. Sorry."

The girl held up her hand, and I was sure she was going to dis Courtney. Instead, she licked her finger and ran it over the tattoo. The black ink smeared. "I got bored during fourth period," she said. "So, can I still try out?"

"You need to fill this out," Whitney told her, holding up a form. "In English." She made like she was talking to a foreigner.

The girl ignored her. "Did it," she said, dropping a piece of paper on our table.

I took a look at it. "Missy, is it?" I asked. "Before we start, I'm afraid we need to make sure you can do a standing back tuck. Standard procedure, you understand." That had scared off more than a couple auditioners. I figured Missy would join them.

"Standing full okay?"

Before I could nod, she executed the cleanest, sharpest, most perfect standing full-twisting back layout I've ever seen.

Yikes. This girl was good.

Whitney extended the challenge. "Brandy, back-handspring, whipback, whipback, tuck out," she demanded, chanting a complex series of moves.

Missy flew into the tumbling pass before Whitney even finished. She hammered it.

"Where is this girl from?" Whitney asked. "Romania? Excuse me, Nadia."

Missy barely glanced at her.

"Can she yell?" asked Courtney.

Missy grinned. "I transferred from Los Angeles!" she hollered, chanting the words. "Your school has no gymnastics team. This is a last resort!" She glanced at Jan and Leslie. "Boy cheerleaders? Wacky."

Jan bristled. "Know this," he told her slowly. "If we had decent football, soccer, or basketball teams we'd be on them. Here. Guys. Cheer. You were asleep, and you just got your wake-up call, all right?"

Missy rolled her eyes.

I took a good look at her. Hmm. Her tumbling skills were righteous, but we'd have to work on the cheering part. I couldn't help challenging her. "Since all our cheers and routines are original, we'll try an oldie," I said. "Try this:

'AwesomeohwowliketotallyfreakmeoutImean-
righton,
the Toros sure are number one!'

Missy paused. "Awesome . . . oh wow . . . like totally . . ." She shook her head. "You busted me. So I've never cheered before, so what? Wouldn't it be weird if I could nail standing fulls, but was, like, totally incapable of memorizing cute rhymes? How about something that actually requires neurons?"

She had a point. And I had to admit I liked her attitude. This girl was feisty.

"Can you stunt, Miss Gymnast?" Courtney asked.

"Sure." Missy gestured to Jan. "C'mon, Cheer Boy." She whispered in his ear. Jan's eyes widened, and he nodded. A nanosecond later, she was flying off his shoulders.

That did it for me. "Missy is bank," I told the others.

"Bank*rupt*!" Courtney insisted. "We have already so decided on Jamie!"

Nobody else spoke up. I had the feeling they were all on her side. Missy was just too much for them. Did I care? "Courtney, this is not a democracy. It's a cheerocracy. I'm sorry, but we're overruling you. That's the royal 'we.'"

She frowned. "You're being a cheer-tator, Torrance. We already voted! Besides, Missy looks more like a roadie for Korn than a cheerleader."

Now it was Missy's turn to frown. "My god, what was I thinking? I cannot walk amongst you people." She made a disgusted face. "Cheerleaders. I have to go wash my hands now." She left the gym, slamming the door behind her.

I whirled on Courtney. "I'm captain, and I'm pulling rank. You can fall in line or not. If we're going to be the best, we have to have the best! And that's Missy."

"Whatever." Courtney glared back.

Now all I had to do was convince Missy.

CHAPTER 8

I didn't take the time to change out of my cheerleading uniform. I just headed straight for the address on Missy's form. I walked up to the front door, rang the bell, and waited.

The door opened.

My jaw dropped.

It was Cliff. The guy from study hall. Only now he was in baggy chinos and a Ramones T-shirt, and he looked, if possible, even cuter than before.

"We don't want any cookies," he said, getting ready to close the door in my face. Clearly he didn't recognize me. Then, suddenly, he did. "Hey, what's with the outfit?"

I glanced down at Missy's application. Sure enough, her last name was right there in big letters. Pantone. How could I have missed that? "Are you —" I began. "I'm —"

Cliff was still staring at my uniform. "A cheerleader . . ." he finished my sentence.

"Head cheerleader, to be exact," I agreed. "Is Missy home?"

"Actually, she moved back to L.A. Something about evil cheerleaders."

I shot him a look. "No, no, we *have* to get her!"

"Are her mood swings going to be a problem?" The guy wouldn't quit.

"Cliff, shut up." Missy had appeared at the door. She rolled her eyes and shrugged. "Big brothers. So, what do you want?" she demanded.

"I want you on the squad." I saw Cliff's eyes widen, but I ignored him. "Look, you're the best and they know it. They just reject the unfamiliar."

"Did you say you want my sister on the squad?" asked Cliff. "You actually refer to yourselves as 'the squad'?"

We both ignored him.

"Thanks but no thanks." Missy sounded definite. "I plead temporary insanity. See, I'm a hardcore gymnast. No way jumping up and down and screaming, 'Go, team, go,' is gonna satisfy me."

I couldn't give up yet. "Look, we're gymnasts, too. Except no beam, no bars, no vault."

"No dice. Not interested." She moved to shut the door. Cliff jammed it open with his arm. She glared at him. "What are you doing?"

"Nothing. I'm just interested in hearing Torrance's point of view."

Missy looked suspicious. "How do you even know her?"

"Aah, we're old friends." Cliff smiled at me.

I smiled back. "Ever been to a cheerleading competition?" I asked Missy.

She shrugged. "Like, a football game?"

She didn't have a clue. "No, not a game. Those are like practices for us. I'm talking about a tournament. ESPN cameras all around. Hundreds of people in the stands cheering."

Cliff interrupted, "People cheering cheerleaders?"

"That's right," I told him, ignoring his sarcastic tone. "Lots of people." I turned to Missy again. "Here's the thing, Missy. We're the deal. The best. We have fun, we work hard, and we win national championships. I'm offering you the chance to be part of that."

"Go for it, Missy," Cliff said, in this fake enthusiastic voice. "Think about it. You get to wear sassy little outfits and yell like you care about something." He looked back at me and shook his head. "She's not the cheering type."

Missy glared at him. Then she looked back at me. "You know what? Count me in."

CHAPTER 9

Missy showed up at practice the next day. I so wanted to show her that she was doing the right thing. I sat her down in the bleachers to watch.

"Ready? Okay!" I called out to the squad. We slammed into our hottest dance routine, the one with fly moves and the most righteous chant:

"I said brrrrr. It's cold in here!
I guess there must be some Toros in the
     atmosphere!
I say brrrr. It's cold in here!
I said there must be some Toros in the
     atmosphere!
I said ice, ice, ice! Ohweohweoh!
Ice, ice, ice! Ohweohweoh!"

The whole thing is over in, like, twenty-five seconds. We hammered it. I snuck a peek at Missy to make sure she was as hugely impressed as she should be.

She didn't look impressed at all.

In fact, she looked mad.

She *was* mad. How could I tell? Oh, maybe it was the way she jumped to her feet and stormed out of the gym.

CHAPTER 10

We all looked at one another other.

"Nice recruit," said Courtney finally. "A real captain would've seen what I saw. A *loser*."

"And she means that in the nicest possible way," snickered Whitney.

She and Courtney tagged up. "I'd say that's strike two," Courtney gloated.

I ran after Missy.

I caught her in the parking lot, just about to climb into her VW Bug. "What's up with you?" I yelled. "I went out on a limb for you, and you just *bail*?"

Missy faced me, hands on hips. "Thieving's not my speed."

Huh? "What are you talking about?"

"You ripped off those cheers." She flipped her car keys and caught them, staring me down.

"Listen, Missy," I protested. "Our cheers are one hundred percent original. Count the trophies!"

"Your trophies are bull, and you're a big fat liar, Captain." She spat out the last word mockingly.

Whoa. I took a step back. Then I stepped forward and got right in her face. "That's right, *Captain*. And I'm not afraid to kick your butt. So get back in there and stop babbling about stolen routines!"

She ignored me and motioned toward her car. "Get in."

"What? No way."

She got into the driver's side and opened the passenger door for me. Now she was smiling. Just a little. "Get in the car. I can see you need a little education."

I hesitated.

"Trust me. Seriously."

I don't know why, but I did. Trust her, I mean. I glanced back toward the gym, then at Missy again. Finally, I sighed and climbed in. She took off out of the parking lot and headed straight onto the freeway, bound for L.A. I watched her drive. Where was she taking me? Had I just gotten into the car of a psychopath? "You're not gonna kill me, are you?"

She just smirked and kept going. We got off at an exit I'd never seen before, and soon we were cruising past a sign that said WELCOME TO THE CITY OF COMPTON.

There was graffiti everywhere, burned-out

buildings, guys hanging out on corners. . . . "Where are you taking me?" I asked. I'd never been anywhere like this before. I mean, I'd seen it in movies and stuff, but that was about it. Nervously, I checked to make sure my door was locked.

"You're not in Kansas anymore, Dorothy," said Missy as she pulled up in front of a sprawling high school with a torn banner out front reading EAST COMPTON CLOVERS.

We got out and she led me into the school, straight to the gym. There was a pep rally going on, and the place was packed. The Clover mascot, a threadbare leprechaun with a droopy four-leaf clover, was jumping around when we came in. Then, just as we squeezed into a spot on the bleachers, everybody started stomping and whistling. The Clovers cheerleading squad was making their entrance.

There were about seven guys and seven girls, all dressed in baggy hip-hop gear. Most of them were African-American or Hispanic, same as the student body filling the bleachers. Laughing and talking, the team strolled in, looking disorganized and laid-back. I glanced at Missy. She arched her eyebrows and mouthed the word *wait*.

One of the girls stepped forward. She had long braids, and her T-shirt read *O Mighty Isis*. She flung her braids back and held up her hands, like a conductor. The squad — and everybody else in the gym — fell silent.

And then:

"I said brrrrr. It's cold in here!
I guess there must be some Clovers in the
 atmosphere!
I say brrrr. It's cold in here!
I said there must be some Clovers in the
 atmosphere!
I said ice, ice, ice! Ohweohweoh!
Ice, ice, ice! Ohweohweoh!"

I couldn't believe my ears.

Or my eyes. Hip-hop music began to blast over the loudspeakers, and the squad started to dance. Their routine was awesome. It was like ours, but way, way beyond it. Original. Fierce. Much, *much* better than anything we'd ever done.

I felt sick.

"Let's go," said Missy. She led me back out of the gym.

We were climbing into her car when I felt a hand grab the collar of my letter jacket. I wrenched myself around and saw Isis, looking even bigger and cooler than she had on the gym floor. Two of the other cheerleaders were with her. According to the embroidery on their jackets, their names were Lava and Jenelope.

"Did you enjoy the show?" Isis asked.

"Yes, were the ethnic festivities to your liking today?" Lava added.

"Y-you guys are awesome," I answered. I was still in shock, and pretty near the point of tears.

"Really?" Isis looked so angry I almost expected sparks to fly out of her eyes. I was shaking. "So are you ready to share those trophies?"

Jenelope shifted on her feet. "Can we just beat these Buffys down so I can get home? I'm on curfew, girl."

I felt my blood turn to ice water.

Missy spoke up. "Look, there's no need for that."

"She's right," said Isis. "We'd be doing them a favor. See, then they could feel good about sending Raggedy Ann down here to rip off our cheers."

"Raggedy Ann?" I didn't know what she was talking about.

"Ugly redhead with a video camera permanently attached to her hand," Isis explained. "You guys have been coming down here and stealing our routines for years."

"And we just love seeing them on ESPN," added Lava.

I still didn't get it. "I don't know what you're talking —"

"Brrr," Isis interrupted, "it's cold in here. There must be some Toros in the atmosphere. You think a white girl made that up?"

"I didn't —"

She held up a hand. "Our free cheer service is over as of this moment."

"O-vah," echoed Jenelope.

"*Finito,*" added Lava.

"Every time we get something, here y'all come stealing it," Isis went on, "puttin' blond hair on it and calling it something different."

I gulped and looked at Missy.

"Our team has been the best for years, but nobody has seen what we can do. I'm gonna change all that. I'm captain this year, and we *will* get to Nationals." Isis held out a hand. "So just hand over the tape you made tonight and we'll call it even for now."

"I — I don't have any tape," I squeaked out.

Missy backed me up. "We just came to see the show."

Isis just looked at us. Out of the corner of my eye I saw the rest of the Clovers approaching. Suddenly I could hardly breathe.

I heard Isis's pals muttering to her. "Come on, Isis." "Let me take care of this."

Isis turned her back on us. "Even if they did steal something," she said, "they won't be able to do it right. And we'll be at Nationals to make sure. Let's go."

"That's it?" asked Jenelope. "We're just gonna let them go?"

"Yes." Isis nodded, and her braids flew around her head. "Unlike them, we have class."

"I swear," I choked out, "I had no idea."

Isis threw me one last look. "Well, now you do." She walked off, leaving me and Missy staring at each other.

Jenelope gave us an evil grin. "You been touched by an angel, girl," she told me. Then she whirled around and followed Isis.

CHAPTER 11

As we pulled away in her Bug, Missy was all exhilaration and relief. "We *so* almost got our butts kicked back there! I knew I'd seen that routine before. We used to play East Compton all the time."

She babbled on, but I didn't respond. I couldn't. I was totally out of it. How could this have happened? There was no denying it. Big Red had totally stolen every single one of our best routines from the Clovers. I felt like throwing up.

Missy turned to look at me. "You really had no idea, did you?" she asked.

I shook my head. "Do you know what this means?" I asked finally, when I could speak again. "My entire cheerleading career has been a lie. Every routine, every trophy . . . a lie."

"Hey, look on the bright side," Missy suggested. "It's only cheerleading."

I sank down in my seat. "*I* am only cheerleading." I knew Missy couldn't possibly understand that. She had, like, this attitude about cheering. But to me, life without cheerleading wouldn't be worth living.

Missy glanced over at me again. I could tell by her eyes that she knew I meant it, even though she couldn't relate. "Can I ask you something?" I sat up again.

"Hit me."

"Do you believe in curses?"

"What are you talking about?" Missy sounded confused.

"I think I'm cursed."

"And why's that?"

And so I told her the whole story, while we drove down the freeway back to San Diego.

It happened last summer, at cheer camp. I had been so psyched to go. It wasn't my first year there, but this time I'd be there as a senior. What could be cooler? There was only one problem: I didn't know about the hazing. Turns out there's a Rancho Carne tradition. Every senior has to go through an induction ritual. And the captain gets to choose what the senior has to do.

I'd hoped Big Red would have mercy on me, but no way (in fact, I don't think the girl knows the meaning of the word). She approached me in the cafeteria one night, in front of the rest of the squad, and told me my mission: I was to capture the Spirit Stick, the very symbol of cheerleading. And drop it. In front of the entire camp.

I felt the sloppy joe I'd just eaten trying to find its way out of my stomach. "But the Spirit Stick can't touch the ground!" I protested. "Everybody knows that. And even if it's a totally bogus concept, it's bad sportsmanship."

Like Big Red cared about sportsmanship. Who did I think I was talking to?

She was firm. "Torrance, the Spirit Stick is not your friend," she said. "In fact, it's what makes people hate cheerleaders. It's girlish and frivolous, and you must rob it of its powers. 'Sportsmen' don't need stupid sticks when they've got discipline and dedication. You're an athlete first, and a cheerleader second. I hope you're not forgetting that. Choose: the squad or the stick."

I looked over at Missy while I told that part. I had a feeling she'd agree with everything Big Red had said. Yup. She was nodding. And in a way, I agreed, too. But the Spirit Stick ... It's still something special, something I can't explain. It has this mystical quality. I couldn't help believing in at least *some* of its legend.

I went on, telling Missy how I'd approached another squad, New Pope. They'd won that night's end-of-camp competition — and the Spirit Stick. They were all smiles. The picture of good sportsmanship. When I came over, the first thing their captain said was that the Toros had been "*such* an inspiration!"

"Um, thanks," I answered. "I just wanted to

congratulate you guys. And get a picture of you, with the Spirit Stick."

They needed no encouragement. In about two seconds flat, they'd built a pyramid. Their coach handed me the Spirit Stick. I held it for a second, making sure Big Red saw it in my hand.

Then I handed it to one of the girls on the second level of the pyramid. I passed it just a *teensy* bit too quickly, accidentally-on-purpose. It fell, as if in slow motion.

Four of the New Pope cheerleaders flew through the air after it, as if they could catch it before it touched the ground. There was screaming, and sobbing, and the Spirit Stick hit the floor with what seemed like a loud crack. Ribbons and sequins flew everywhere.

Suddenly, the cafeteria fell silent. Every single cheerleader in the place was staring at me. Me, Torrance Shipman, who will go down in history as The Girl Who Dropped the Spirit Stick.

I bent to pick it up. Then I went to hand it to a New Pope cheerleader. She shrank from it. "I don't want it now," she said.

"It's okay," another girl on her squad said. "It's fine. The Spirit Stick doesn't lose anything." She was hyperventilating a little, trying to convince herself that what she was saying was true. "But the person who drops it," she paused, and her voice got lower, "is *cursed.* Forever."

As I finished the story, I heard peals of laughter. I turned to see Missy cracking up. How *could* she?

"I don't mean to laugh, Torrance," she said, shaking her head. "But it sounds to me like an urban legend. A cheerleading urban legend."

I raised my eyebrows.

"You're not jinxed," she assured me. "Stuff happens. Forget about it."

I wish I could.

CHAPTER 12

I had to talk to Aaron. He would understand. He would help me.

As soon as I got back home, I dashed for the phone.

Justin came in while I was in the middle of dialing. "I have to tell you something," he said.

"I'm on the phone, creep!" As if it weren't obvious.

"I realize that," Justin said, smiling. "And normally, I'd be on the other line. But this is important."

"Okay, what?" I asked. (Am I a saint, or what?)

Justin let out a loud, long belch.

"Oh, gross!" I cried.

Justin grinned. "Thank you for listening," he said.

"Get out!" Could my life get any worse? As he left the room, I finished dialing. "Hello?" I asked his roommate. "Is Aaron around?"

He wasn't.

I left a message, classified "urgent."

CHAPTER 13

"I mean, Big Red really messed us up. Big time. And I'm gonna put this to the entire squad: Swear you guys didn't know."

Practice, the next day. I'd just spilled the whole story about seeing the Clovers do "our" routine.

"No way!" "Uh-uh." "Are you kidding?" They all denied knowledge.

"She didn't exactly let any of us help her with the routines, Torrance," Jan reminded me.

"I just can't believe it," murmured Leslie.

I couldn't stop ranting. "I feel hideous. It's depraved! That East Compton girl wanted to beat me up. And I can't blame her."

Darcy gave me a sympathetic look. "Big Red ran the show, man. We were just the flying ignorami, for sobbing out loud."

Leslie backed her up. "She's right. We had zero clue, Tor."

"Yeah!" "For real." "Word." Everybody agreed.

It was time to drop the next bombshell. "We

can't go to Regionals with a stolen routine," I told them. I'd made that decision the night before, as I lay there sleepless. "It's too risky."

Whitney nearly jumped out of her skin. "Changing the routine now would be total murder-suicide!" she gasped.

"Really," Courtney agreed (how unusual). "Let's not put the *duh* in dumb. So, how do we deal with it? We do what anyone in this situation would do."

I could hardly wait to hear her solution.

She and Whitney exchanged a glance. Together, they chanted, "We ignore it."

Darcy nodded in agreement. "How's East Compton gonna prove anything? What're they gonna do?" She put on a girly voice and pointed dramatically. "They stole! Revoke their license!"

Missy was standing next to me, and I could practically see the steam coming out of her ears. Finally, she blew. "You guys are unbelievable! You're talking about cheating here."

Courtney rolled her eyes. "Sorry, new girl. No-body hit your buzzer." She turned to me. "Look, I hate to be predictable, but guess what? I just don't care. We learned the routine fair and square. We logged the man-hours. Don't punish the squad for Big Red's mistake." She stood up a little straighter and got all dramatic. "This is *not* about cheating. This is about winning!" She raised her hand. "Everyone in favor of winning?"

I looked around at each person on the squad. I could tell they were in dire need of leadership. Nobody knew what to do. The last person I looked at was Missy. I hated to disappoint her. And I agreed with her, totally. But there was no denying that Courtney had a point. "I get what you're saying," I told Missy. "But it's just too late. If we don't do the routine we've worked on, we've got nothing."

The disappointment in her eyes nearly made me choke.

"Stuff happens," Jan added. "And you deal with it, you know? So, are you in?" He knew, as I did, that we needed her badly. She was our flyer, after all.

Missy hesitated. I knew she wasn't happy with where this was going. The rest of the squad fell silent. Missy was on the spot. "Whatever," she said, finally.

Missy was in.

Only problem? I knew, and she knew, that she needed work on her stunting. She knew how to leap and tumble on her own but not how to do a lot of the other stunts we do, like balancing on one another's shoulders and basically flying into the air. She agreed to an extra practice later that day and invited me, Leslie, and Jan over to her house to work out. "We have a huge backyard," she said. "Plenty of room to throw me around."

Which is exactly what Jan and Leslie started to do, a few hours later.

After her third try at a Liberty — a stunt where the cheerleader strikes a Lady Liberty pose while three other cheerleaders hold her up — Missy was still having trouble. "This stunting stuff is scary," she said.

"What's the big deal?" asked Leslie. "You fall, we catch."

Missy shook her head. "Remember, I'm a gymnast. In my world, you fall, you fall."

"That's why cheerleading rules," said Leslie.

Jan tried to explain. "Just grip this," he said. "You don't know me. Theoretically it would be impossible for you to trust me yet. But trust me. Not only will I not drop you, but the mere knowledge of my presence will make you not want to fall."

Deep.

"Okay," Missy said. "Let's do it."

That time, they almost hit it. It wasn't perfect, but it was much, much better. But Missy was still skeptical. "This whole stunting thing is stupid," she said. "And if we win with this routine, we're like Milli Vanilli accepting the Grammy."

Jan and Leslie exchanged a puzzled look, but I knew who she was talking about. That singing duo from the eighties who turned out to be total lip-synchers.

"Spare us the sermon," Jan told her. "When you feel how sore you are tomorrow, multiply that by a hundred and you'll start to realize how much work we've already put into this routine. If you still want to change it after that, let us know."

They went back to work. I decided to take a break. "Can I get something to drink in your kitchen?" I asked Missy.

Distracted, she waved a hand in my direction. I headed inside.

Clearly, the Pantone family had not quite finished settling in. The kitchen floor was littered with boxes marked COOKBOOKS, LADLES, ETC., and BEST CHINA.

I opened the fridge and spotted a carton of orange juice. Pulling it out, I looked around for a glass. The cabinets were a jumble of cereal boxes and canned soup, but there wasn't a tumbler in sight. I glanced behind me, just to make sure nobody was peeking. Then, shrugging, I opened the carton and took a swig.

"Classy."

The o.j. almost came out my nose. I turned to see Cliff over in the corner, nearly hidden by a stack of boxes.

Busted.

well . . . all," I rolled my eyes. "Now we what . . . the orange here now? I know the words to my . . . Well . . . I think I saw . . . You see it . . .

CHAPTER 14

"**H**ey, what are you, spying on me?" I figured my best defense was a good offense. I put the carton down on the counter and moved in front of it, trying to hide it.

Cliff emerged from behind the boxes. He was smiling. His smile made me feel . . . something. "This happens to be our kitchen. And you're the one putting her backwash into our orange juice, so I wouldn't go casting aspersions."

"Okay," I admitted, "so you caught me drinking from the carton. Is that, like, a capital crime?"

Cliff shrugged. "No, it's just that it's not the kind of behavior one might expect from the head cheerleader."

That again. I tossed my head at him. "You don't like cheerleaders much, do you?" I asked.

"I guess I haven't thought about it," he said carelessly.

"No?"

"In fact, I think you're the first actual cheerleader I've met."

"Oh, really?" I raised my eyebrows. "So, what do you make of me?" I honestly wanted to know.

"Well." Cliff looked thoughtful. "You seem . . . oh . . . cheerful?"

Gimme a break. "Nice. What else?"

He grinned. "Thirsty?"

"No, *really*." Suddenly, it really mattered to me. What he thought.

He was quiet for a second. "Really?"

"Yeah."

"The truth?"

"Yeah."

"No bull, really cut-through-to-it, straight-on-the-level kinda honesty?"

"Yeah!" That's exactly what I wanted.

He looked right into my eyes. "I think," he said slowly, "I think I'm completely into you."

The words just hung there for a moment. I was, like, stunned.

"I think." He added the words as an afterthought.

"I have a boyfriend." Immediately, I wanted to smack myself. Why did I have to say that?

Cliff considered this. "You don't look at me like you have a boyfriend," he said softly.

I had to snap out of it. I shook myself. "I should go back out there and help them. Thanks for the — uh — juice." I stammered. I turned and walked away. I didn't even want to think about the expression on his face.

CHAPTER 15

The only trouble was, I couldn't *stop* thinking about it. I still had the image of Cliff's face in my mind that night, even while I was speed-dialing Aaron over and over, trying to get through. His phone had been busy for, like, hours.

Justin and I were in the living room. Justin was "doing his homework," which meant he was playing Sega with an open book in front of him. I was "working on my college applications," which meant I was ignoring the stack on the coffee table.

I hit speed dial again. Busy. "Get out of here," I told Justin, taking out my frustration on my innocent little brother.

"Hey, this is the living room. It's public domain." He didn't budge.

I hit speed dial again. This time the phone rang. And then a voice came over the speakerphone. It wasn't Aaron's. "Yo," it said.

I grabbed the phone. "May I please speak to Aaron? It's Torrance."

"He's not home. Buh-bye!"

Click.

The dial tone seemed extra loud. I moved the phone away from my ear and stared at it, annoyed. Justin cracked up.

"I'll take Famous Losers for two hundred, Alex," he said.

"Shut up. It's not my fault —"

"That you're in love with a big dopey cheerleader-guy who won't take your calls?" Justin asked.

"Listen, you, he's just busy." I didn't want to argue about it. It wasn't so easy to defend Aaron when I hadn't talked to him in over a week.

I reached over and pulled the plug on Justin's Sega, ending his game. He called me a name and left. I had about two seconds of peace, and then my mom came in. She sat down, picked up the stack of college applications, and started to leaf through them. "What are these?" she asked, all innocence.

"College applications." Duh.

"Eastern Memphis?" she asked. "University of Southern Kentucky? Are you planning to join the Confederacy?"

I should have known she'd have something to say about it. I tried to be patient. "I'm eligible for cheerleading scholarships at both of those colleges," I explained.

"Dear God."

My dad came in and joined us, glancing at the papers my mom held. "You know," he began carefully, "we have totally supported you in this endeavor —"

"Endeavor?" Jeez. "It's a *sport*." How many times was I going to have to explain this to them?

"We know you think so," my mother said, in her most soothing tones. "And we do acknowledge that it has some" — she cleared her throat "— sportlike qualities. But where's the future in it? The Laker Girls?"

I nearly choked. She really knew how to get to me. Through clenched teeth, I said, "What we do is nothing like the Laker Girls, and if you'd come to a competition once in a while you wouldn't think that it was. And why are you so obsessed with the future? This is who I am right now! This is what I love."

Mom turned to Dad. "She's gone, honey. Completely." She threw up her hands.

Dad took over. "Okay, look," he said, doing his I-can-be-reasonable thing. "I think I can get your mom to entertain your top college choices. But you have to work with me, honey. Let's deal."

I was feeling stubborn. "I am not cutting a deal on my college experience!" I told him. "It's my four years, isn't it?"

My father considered this. "Not really, no. This is more of a limited partnership. So, we'll give you Southern Kentucky, Eastern Memphis, and South Carolina if you agree to apply to . . ." He thought for a second. "Let's say UCLA, Berkeley, or Pomona. And that is an excellent deal, I'd say." He leaned back and folded his arms.

I snorted. "Pomona? They don't even have a mascot, let alone a cheering squad!"

"Yes, they do!" my mother put in. "The Sagehens."

That just about put me over the edge. "Are you kidding me? I am not cheering for the Sagehens. That's —"

My dad interrupted. "Torrance, do we have a deal?" He extended his hand.

I saw no way out. What could I do? I sighed. "Deal," I said, shaking on it.

CHAPTER 16

"**O**ooh, *baby*!"

"Lookin' hot!"

"You go, girl!" I leaned out the window of Leslie's Wagoneer and joined him and Jan in admiring Missy. She was standing on the front steps of her house, looking uncertain. She was dressed in her Toros uniform for the first time, and we were picking her up on our way to her first night game.

She gave us this doubtful look, like, "Really?"

We whistled and cheered some more.

Finally, Missy broke into a grin. She was blushing, which made her look totally cute. She did a few dance steps for us, then ran to hop in beside me.

"Are you psyched?" I asked. I was making some final notes in the game notebook I keep, where I plan which routines we'll do.

"I guess." She looked doubtful.

"You should be," I told her. "I am. This is your big introduction as our new squad member."

"Don't remind me." She looked pale.

I decided to change the subject. "You sure it's okay if I stay at your house tonight?"

"Totally fine. The 'rents are at some benefit. They won't be home till late."

"Cool," I said. I gave her a big smile. "We gotta start practicing early tomorrow. But for now let's go out there and enjoy ourselves. You'll be a star cheerleader yet!"

"All the cheerleaders in the world would not help our football team," Jan muttered from the front seat.

"It's just wrong," Leslie agreed. "Cheering for them is just plain mean. It makes it even more painfully obvious what losers they are."

"Everybody comes to watch you ladies anyway," said Jan, turning in his seat to look at Missy and me.

"Right," Missy deadpanned. "Because we're such fine athletes."

She still wasn't convinced that cheerleading was a sport. I was going to have to keep working on her.

"Wait till you see how much the crowd appreciates us," I told her.

She looked skeptical, but afterward I know even she had to admit that we got a lot more attention than the football players that night.

We arrived on time and I gathered the squad

for a quick pep talk. Then we waited off the field while the announcer introduced the football team. "Now, ladies and gentlemen, put your hands together for the Rancho Carne To-roooos!"

The stands were full, but there was only a brief smattering of applause as the team stormed the field, pumping their fists in the air.

"And now," boomed the announcer's voice again, "without further ado, let's hear it for the five-time national cheerleading champions: the mighty To-rooooos!"

We charged onto the field, full steam ahead, whooping and hollering and jumping and clapping. The pep band started up, drums beating and horns blaring.

The crowd went berserk. Everybody in the stands leaped to their feet and there was a roar of approval.

For us.

The cheerleaders.

I love it.

I glanced over at Missy. Was she loving it, too? Uh-oh. She had that "deer in the headlights" look. I waited until she met my eyes and gave her a smile and an encouraging nod. She could do it! I knew she could. She just had to give herself a little attitude adjustment.

I smiled at her again as I led the squad in a series of jumps. Finally, Missy gave this little "oh, well" kind of shrug and threw herself into it, jumping higher and smiling bigger than anyone else on the squad.

Excellent.

I gave her an approving nod. Then I turned to gaze up at the stands, just to check out who was there, and right away I spotted Cliff. He was staring at Missy with this unbelieving look on his face. As I watched, he shook his head, pulled out a book, and began to read.

Grrr . . .

I decided to ignore him. Instead, I watched as the two teams took to the field. From my spot on the sidelines, I could hear the captains giving each other a hard time as they met for the coin toss.

"Repeat after me," said the captain of the other team, "I'm a big, fat, football-playing joke."

His cocaptain snickered. "Why don't you just let your cheerleaders play for you?" he added. "At least they win stuff occasionally."

Then, just before the game began, the other team's seven cheerleaders came out and performed a lame "hello" cheer, mixing in a few insults as they greeted us. I whispered to the squad and we exploded with a response:

"That's all right, that's okay,
You're gonna pump our gas someday!"

Then the game started, and so did the carnage. Our players took one hard hit after another. I could hardly stand to watch. So I did what I do best: I cheered. No matter how lame our team is, we're there to support them. I led the squad through a few routines, but I have to admit I was pretty distracted knowing that Cliff was there watching. Every time we started a cheer, he looked up from his book and paid close attention. And every time I saw him looking, I looked right back. It was almost as if nobody else existed, in the stands or on the field.

As we finished a cheer and trooped back to the sidelines, Whitney hissed into my right ear, "You're, like, totally his eye candy!"

Courtney approached from the left. "God, I can't believe you'd do that to Aaron!" She shook her head.

"Do what?" I asked.

They rolled their eyes. "Especially with him," Whitney said, wrinkling her nose as if she were smelling cat pee.

"I don't know what you're —" I began.

"Don't play dumb," Whitney told me as they strolled away. "We know what you're up to."

My face was still red with embarrassment when we headed out for our next cheer. But it must have turned white when I looked at the sidelines. I was in midchant when I noticed the Clovers walk in, filling up a front row. What

were they doing here? I had a bad feeling about
this.

I looked over at Missy.

She looked back at me, eyes wide.

Yikes.

We kept on with our cheer. What else could
we do?

> "Allll right! We're sweet!
> We got the whip, we can't be beat!
> We're the best, our team's too cool.
> We got the class to rock this school!"

We were on the last line of that chant when
the Clovers cut us off. They lined up in forma-
tion, facing us.

> "Aaaaw, yeah! We bad!
> We got the team we can't be had!
> We're the best, so score them points.
> You win the game, we'll rock this joint!"

Within seconds, all attention was riveted on
the showdown on the sidelines. The game didn't
stop, but it might as well have. Nobody, including
the other team's cheerleaders, was paying the
least bit of attention to what was happening on
the field. All eyes were on us — and on the
Clovers. I gritted my teeth and called for another
chant. We began to step and clap.

"Toros, go, Toros! Yo, yo, go, Toros!"

We were tight, and I knew it. Looking good. But then Isis led her squad into an even tighter, stepping routine.

"Clovers, go, Clovers! Yo, yo, go, Clovers!"

Every move we tried, the Clovers gave us back. And they did everything better. *Way* better. No question about it. The fans knew it, too. They were staring at the Clovers, amazed.

What could I do? I kept whipping the squad along.

"Our game is fierce and we are hip
So get on back you can't touch this —"

The Clovers interrupted, not even letting us finish.

"Our game is bad, we're without peer
So get that weak mess out of here!"

Finally, I gave in. We couldn't keep up. We were out of breath, out of rhymes, out of moves. The Clovers were stomping our butts. We just stood there, dazed, as Isis raised her arms and led her squad in one last burst of cheering.

"Tried to steal our bit
But you look like — !
We're the real deal.
You can't deny it.
You a little worry.
We're a full-scale panic!
You a rowboat.
And we're the ship 'Titanic!'
We're the ocean.
You just a little rain puddle.
You a paper plane.
And we're the real space shuttle!
O-R-I-G-I-N-A-L
The real deal, we're original!"

They ended the cheer in perfect unison, each one of them giving each one of *us* an icy stare.

Then Isis flashed a nasty smile at me. "This is just a sample of what will be waiting for you at Nationals," she said.

Lava nodded in agreement. "An ignominious *aperitif*!" she added. (She must use the same SAT study book as Darcy.)

Jenelope looked confused for a moment. Then she nodded. "Whatever that means, *yeah*!" she said.

"Watch yo' back," Isis said flatly. Then she led her squad out of the stadium, without a backward glance.

Gulp.

My squad was staring at me. Like, what was I supposed to say?

Courtney was the first to snap out of it. "I *still* say we use the routine we have!"

At that moment, the final buzzer sounded. The game was over. I glanced up at the scoreboard. It read 21–0. What else is new?

When I looked back at the squad, everybody was staring at Courtney as if she were out of her mind. She set her jaw, stubborn. "If we have to start over, I quit!" she said.

Whatever. It was time to make a decision. I stepped forward. "Whoever here is for a new routine, raise your hand."

Everybody on the squad, except Courtney, raised their hands. And so did *all* the people in the stands.

That was it. It was time to make a change.

CHAPTER 17

"**S**o? Your first big game. How'd it feel?"
Back at the Pantone residence, Missy and I were in her room, getting ready for bed. I plumped up the pillow she'd tossed me.

"Well," Missy said, pretending to consider, "except for the part when those East Compton girls made us look like thieving morons, and when our team lost by three touchdowns, and when I got thrown all over the place for two hours . . . pretty good."

I waved a hand. "You'll get used to it," I told her. Then I heard it. The sound of a guitar. I felt like a dog who hears his master's whistle: My ears perked up and my head turned automatically toward the door. "I — I better go brush my teeth."

I headed down the hallway, peeking into rooms as I passed them. The guitar riffs grew louder. And then, suddenly, I was staring into Cliff's room. Staring at Cliff, to be exact. He sat on the bed, intent on the electric guitar in his

Unlike Aaron, Cliff really believes in Torrance. But he gets angry when Torrance blows him off after Regionals.

Whitney, Isis, Torrance, and Missy . . .

. . . strut their stuff!

All that practice pays off at Nationals. The Toros' new routine rocks! Torrance and Missy know they nailed it ... but is it enough to win?

Isis and the Clovers celebrate their own
original routine.

In the end, Cliff realizes that cheerleader or not, Torrance is the only one for him. And, uh, vice versa!

hands. He was playing something sort of punky, not that I know my musical eras all that well. The important thing was, it sounded soulful and intense, and Cliff was totally into it. I watched his strong hands moving over the strings.

"What are you doing?"

I jumped and turned to see Missy standing there, hands on her hips. As I moved, I banged into Cliff's door, and the guitar riff broke off.

He looked at me.

I looked at him.

He was smiling.

"I — um — where's the bathroom?" I asked.

Missy gave me a weird look. "Right there," she said, pointing down the hall.

I nodded, dazed. I gave Cliff one last glance, then walked away.

A minute later, as I was brushing my teeth, Cliff joined me at the sink. He didn't say a word; he just reached for the toothpaste, unscrewed the cap very deliberately, and squeezed some Aqua-Fresh onto a purple toothbrush. He turned on the water.

I put my hand beneath the faucet, caught some water, rinsed, and turned off the faucet.

He turned it back on.

I rinsed some more, and turned it off.

I spat into the sink.

Then he spat.

He rinsed again, spat again, wiped his mouth

on a green towel, and gave me this huge smile. Without saying a word, he put down his tooth-brush and left.

You're just going to have to believe me on this: The whole episode was incredibly romantic. I know. It sounds kind of gross. But it wasn't. It was — beautiful.

When I stumbled my way back into Missy's room, still in a daze, she was waiting for me, propped up on her elbows in bed. "Are you into my brother?" she asked.

Yes.

"No! I have a boyfriend." I reached over and switched out the light. Then I crawled into bed and lay there smiling, thinking of Cliff.

CHAPTER 18

I slept like a rock. But the second I woke up, I remembered what had happened at the game the night before. The Clovers were serious about coming to Nationals. That meant they'd be at Regionals, for sure. And if we showed up with their routine, we were going to be laughed right out of the competition.

I rolled over and reached for the phone on Missy's night table. It was early. Aaron *had* to be in his room. I punched in the number.

"Aaron?" I asked. I saw Missy's eyes open. She watched me, interested.

"Tor?" Aaron sounded groggy. "Is that you? It's kinda early. . . ."

"Where have you been?" I asked. "I've been trying to call you." His voice sounded so familiar. I'd almost forgotten how deep it was. I could picture him, lying in bed with rumpled hair and sleepy eyes.

"Yeah, I know." He yawned. "I'm sorry. I've

been, like, totally busy with school and practice and stuff. What's up?"

"It's bad, Aaron. Miss Red snaked our routines from the East Compton Clovers. *All* our routines!" The story spilled out.

"What?" Aaron was waking up by then.

"And they found out," I went on. "They showed up at our game. Gauntlets were thrown. Tell me you didn't know about this!" I felt panicky. "I mean, I don't know what to do here!"

"Of course I didn't know! But you gotta calm down." Aaron's voice turned soothing. "It's not that big of a deal. Everybody uses everybody's material. It's, like, an unwritten rule or something."

Missy was still watching. I knew she was dying to know what Aaron was saying. "That doesn't help me!" I cried. "We can't do their routine at Regionals because *they're* gonna do their routine at Regionals."

Aaron's voice turned from soothing to slightly impatient. "Hey, c'mon, Tor, it's me. I don't think you need to go all 911 here. You need a new routine, that's all. No problem. Just hire a professional choreographer."

"A choreographer?"

Missy stared at me.

"No way! We'll get busted!"

"I don't think so," Aaron said. "Everyone does it, anyway. The UCA totally looks the other way."

Could that be true? I'd always thought the Universal Cheerleading Association was, like, completely strict. Call me naive. "What do you mean everyone?" I demanded.

"Southern Kentucky and U. of Eastern Memphis, to name a few." Aaron sounded totally sure of himself.

"Southern Kentucky and U. of Eastern Memphis? No way!" The squads at those schools are awesome.

"Every which!" Aaron insisted. "Look, just think of it as a collaboration. Call this choreographer dude. His name's Sparky Polastri. I met him at Nationals last year. He knows his stuff. Here's his number."

I gestured to Missy for a pen. She grabbed one off her desk and handed it over. I scribbled down the number Aaron gave me. "Okay, thanks. Aaron, you always make things better. Bye! Call me." I hung up, just catching sight of Missy making a "don't make me sick" face.

She was pulling on a T-shirt as I climbed out of bed. "He says we should hire a choreographer," I reported, as if she hadn't heard.

Missy frowned. "I know I'm the new girl, but that sounds like a bad call."

I glanced at the paper in my hand. Then I

reached for the phone and dialed. "Well, stick with me, new girl, and I'll show you how things work." The phone rang, and somebody picked up. "Hello," I said. "May I please speak to Sparky Polastri?"

CHAPTER 19

"He says he needs three or four days to teach us the routine," I told Kasey and Darcy the next day. Talking to Sparky had sold me on the idea of hiring a choreographer. He sounded confident, energetic, and very upbeat. The Toros' morale was at a very low point; we could use an infusion of new blood. I had high hopes that Sparky was our man. "But here's the thing," I went on. "It's gonna cost two thousand dollars."

Kasey and I both looked at Darcy.

"What?" she asked. "Do I have the letters A-T-M tattooed on my forehead?"

"We were thinking more like D-A-D-D-Y," I said. Darcy's dad is loaded, and he treats his little girl like the princess she is.

Darcy thought about it. "Maybe I could get five hundred."

"Okay!" I said. It was a beginning. "So we only need fifteen hundred more by Monday."

Time to start thinking. How could we earn that much money, quickly?

CHAPTER 20

A car wash, two bake sales, and a phone drive later, I counted up the cash we'd earned. "A thousand nine-hundred eighty, and —" I threw down one last twenty. "Two grand! We did it." I was psyched.

Courtney wasn't. "Where is this guy?" she asked impatiently as she did a forward bend.

We were in the school's rehearsal room, waiting for Sparky Polastri. He wasn't really that late, only half an hour. And we needed to warm up, anyway. "Listen," I told Courtney. "We're lucky he's even doing this for us." Just then, there was a knock at the door. I ran to throw it open. My smile faded when I saw Sparky standing there.

He was a big, buff, macho-looking guy, like something out of one of those old synth bands from the '80s. He was dressed all in black, with huge biker boots. He brushed past me, stalked into the room, and set down the huge boom box he was carrying. Without a word, he reached down to press play, and cheesy-sounding music filled the room. Sparky began to dance in this really dramatic way, all thrusts and poses. He looked deadly serious, which may have been the only thing keeping me from giggling. Was he for real? Finally, the song reached a climax. "Prepare for total domination!" screamed the singer. Sparky struck one last pose, then walked over and turned off the boom box.

We just stood there, dazed. I couldn't look at anyone else. Then Sparky walked toward our little group. "Thanks for coming," I said, finally finding my voice. "We —"

He held up a hand. "Don't speak." He walked down the ragged line we'd formed on the floor, coming first to Kasey. "You. You have weak ankles." Next was Courtney. "One of your calves is bigger than the other."

Kasey looked appalled.

Courtney looked outraged.

"Too much makeup," Sparky went on, going on down the line. "Not enough makeup." He got to Whitney. "What's with the skin?" he asked. "Say it with me: 'sunlight.'"

Whitney's jaw dropped open.

But Sparky was already looking at Jan and Leslie. "Male cheerleaders? 'Nuff said." He approached Darcy. "Good general tone and musculature."

Darcy looked smug. Then Sparky walked behind her and went on, "But you better report those compliments to your butt before it gets so big it starts its own website."

I was about to give Darcy a sympathetic glance when Sparky whirled to face me. "And you," he said, "I take it you're captain. Which means you probably need the most work of all."

"Look," I began. "You don't have to —"

He held up that hand again. "Shh, shh, shh, shh, shh!"

"But —" Where did this guy get off, acting this way?

"No, no, no," Sparky said. "Quiet. Don't speak, don't think. Listen and learn. I am a choreographer, and that's what I do. You are cheerleaders. Cheerleaders are dancers who have lost their brains. What you do is a tiny pathetic subset of dancing. I will attempt to transform your robotic routines into poetry written with the human body. Follow me or perish, sweater monkeys."

I gulped. This was *not* what I had expected. I felt the others glaring at me. What could I do? We'd hired the guy. We were going to have to see it through. And maybe he could help us, if we survived his insults.

Sparky walked over and hit play again. The cheesy music blared out. Nobody moved a muscle. He turned to face us. "Now, spread out. When you stand that close together the terrible is too concentrated."

I cringed, knowing that the others were going

to kill me. Then I did what I had to do. I threw myself into the session with Sparky. If I was going to be the squad's leader, I had to make an example of myself.

A couple of hours later, we were still at it. Sparky had created a routine that involved a really tough maneuver where Missy was practically spinning in the air above us. "No!" he cried as we tried it for the eighth time. "More spin! More height! I want to feel like she might drop and snap her neck!"

Nice.

Jan tossed Missy up once more. She slipped — and he caught her. By the shorts. Missy frowned at him.

"I told you I'd catch you," Jan said.

She gave him a swat.

Sparky led us through the routine one last time. I was so tired I could barely think, much less move. Finally, we marched toward Sparky, holding out our hands in corny "spirit fingers," the way he'd shown us.

He stood up and smashed his chair against the floor. It broke into pieces. We stopped moving. "These are not spirit fingers!" he ranted, imitating our hand movements. "*These* are spirit fingers!" He did them again, much more dramatically. "And these are *gold*!"

I was too exhausted to do anything but copy the stupid spirit fingers — and hope he was right.

CHAPTER 21

I was still hoping a couple of days later, while Missy and I practiced in her backyard. We went through the steps of the dance part of the routine over and over, and every time we did it I got more and more depressed.

The routine was lame.

There was no getting around it. I knew it, and so did Missy. But what could we do? We were stuck with it. We'd paid Sparky every cent we could scrape together, so there was no more money. And Regionals were only days away, so there was no more time, either.

"Forget this!" Missy finally said, after one last attempt to make the routine seem less totally cheesy than it was. "I didn't sign on for spirit fingers!" She threw up her hands and headed for the house.

"Missy! C'mon! The spirit fingers are great!" What was I *saying*? What a mess. I stood there for a second, shaking my head. Then, slowly, I crossed over to the old, rusty swing set that sat in the Pantones' backyard. I settled into one of the swings and just sat there, thinking.

"Are they doing construction on your house or something?"

I looked up to see Cliff standing there. I guess he was cracking on how often I'd been over lately. Ha-ha. "Hey," I said.

"What's the matter?" He looked genuinely concerned.

"You don't want to know," I told him.

"Ah, cheer crisis." He lifted an eyebrow.

I shook my head. "How'd I get so bogged down in all this crap?"

Cliff didn't answer right away. Instead, he walked behind me and started to push me on the swing. The last time anyone did that, I must have been about five years old. There was something very comforting about it. "If it's crap," he said from behind me, "why do you do it?"

I thought for a second. "I don't know," I said honestly. If he'd asked me that a month ago, I would have said it was because I loved cheering. But lately, I wasn't so sure.

"So, quit." Cliff gave me an extra little shove, and the swing took off.

"Maybe I should." I pumped my legs to make myself go even higher.

He kept pushing. "If you don't like it any-more . . ."

"I didn't say that!"

"Sounds like it." Could he read my mind or something?

I stopped pumping, and the swing slowed down. "I don't know what I want."

Cliff was silent for a second. I wondered what he was thinking. I wondered if he knew what *I* was thinking: that not knowing what I wanted anymore included not knowing if I wanted Aaron — or Cliff.

Finally, he spoke again. "Listen, I remember when I cheered at my school in Detroit —"

"What?" I twisted around to look at him, and felt the swing veer crookedly to one side. "You cheered at your other school?"

He was smiling. "No," he admitted. "I never cheered. But I know what you're going through. And regardless of the politics and the doubts and all the junk —" He leaned in closer. I was still twisted around, facing him. The swing had stopped by then. "You just have to know you can do it."

I looked at him. His face was very, very close to mine.

"And if it helps," he went on, his voice growing softer, "*I* know you can do it."

"You do?"

He nodded and leaned in even closer. We were so close at that moment.

So close.

And then — he was even closer. He was going

to kiss me, I knew it. Any second now, he was going to do it. And I . . . I was going to let him.

"Okay! Let's do this!" Missy bounded back out of the house, flashing spirit fingers and a huge smile.

Cliff leaned back. I hopped up off the swing. The mood was broken.

It was probably just as well. Aaron, you know.

Missy struck a pose. "Regionals, here we come!" she cried, giving it every ounce of enthusiasm she could fake.

CHAPTER 22

"**W**elcome to the world of competitive cheerleading!" I smiled encouragingly at Missy, who looked completely disoriented.

"What?" she yelled.

I shook my head. "Never mind." It was too hard to try to communicate over the din of dozens of hyper cheerleaders. I looked around, trying to see things through Missy's eyes. I'd been to so many competitions that I'd forgotten how it must feel to see it all for the first time.

A huge banner hung over the entrance to the arena: UCA WELCOMES CALIFORNIA STATE REGIONALS! As a river of cheer squads of all ages flowed by, an event coordinator stood there directing traffic. She read off her clipboard, talking faster than I thought humanly possible. "Youth Cheer, Youth All-Star, Youth Pom, and Youth Novelty, move to the left! High school divisions — check the signs if you don't hear your division — Junior High, Junior Varsity, Small, Medium, and Large Varsity All-Girl, move right! Small and Large Varsity

Coed, straight back to the rehearsal tent! All Pom, Jazz, HighKick, Prop, Crowd Leading, and Mascot contestants need to reregister out front!"

Whoa.

I moved through the crowd, registering momentary glimpses of the World of Cheer: a squad kneeling in a circle, praying; three cheerleaders silently mouthing their cheers while doing spastic little shorthand movements as they visualized their routines; Courtney yelling at a Tiny Tot cheerleader who was trying to cut in line at the ladies' room.

On the main stage up front, a Pee-Wee All-Star squad was performing. One of the girls' moms was shrieking at a judge. "Hey, you. Yes. Your head was down. Your head was down during that move! How are you going to give a proper score if you're not looking." She finished with a threat. "I'm watching you!" Then she turned back to watch her daughter. "Go, Gators!" she screamed.

Jan and Les were walking in front of me and Missy. Jan was checking out every single female cheerleader. "Hi," he'd say. "My name's Jan. Rancho Carne Toros." If the girl didn't react, he'd try again. "Five-time National Champion Rancho Carne Toros?"

Leslie just laughed at him as girl after girl brushed on by.

Next to us, I heard Darcy give Kasey some

last-minute advice. "Remember, they give extra points for alacrity and effulgence."

"Did we bring those?" asked Kasey, clueless as always.

Darcy didn't answer. I looked at her and saw her staring to her right. There, heading our way, were the Clovers. Isis was leading the way as they strutted confidently through the crowd. "Oh, no," said Darcy. "Look who's here."

Kasey shot Isis a smile. "Hi!" she said tentatively.

Isis just nodded as the Clovers cruised by.

"We're in trouble," Darcy muttered.

A half hour later, I knew she was right. As the announcer introduced the Clovers — "in their first-ever appearance at the California Regionals" — their music started up. A heavy, funky bass line filled the arena as the Clovers exploded onto the stage. Missy and I were right up front, with the rest of our squad. The Clovers were *rockin'*. The crowd was going wild. I saw Whitney's face turn stark white, no easy task with that tan. Even Kasey started cheering along with the rest of the crowd — until Darcy kicked her.

The music thumped on, the Clovers got down, and my heart started to feel as heavy as lead. I sneaked a peek at the judges. They looked as enthralled as everyone else. Finally, the routine ended with an amazing stunt.

"Wow," said Jan.

"We are so paling in their shadow," Whitney said.

Courtney frowned. "Paling? We're disappearing."

I thought of our massively inane routine and groaned. Just then, someone tapped me on the shoulder. "Torrance Shipman?"

I turned to see a television reporter, with a cameraman behind her. "You're the new captain of the Rancho Carne Toros, right?" she asked. "Do you have time for a quick interview?"

I gulped. "Sure," I said. I led her backstage with the rest of the squad.

I tried to project confidence when the camera was aimed at me, but I know I didn't succeed. Instead, I was projecting pure, cold fear. With a smile, of course. I'm a cheerleader.

"I'm here with five-time national returning champions, the Rancho Carne Toros!" The reporter was upbeat. So was my squad. Or at least they appeared that way. They whooped and hollered behind me.

"Leading the squad this year is senior Torrance Shipman." She turned to me. "Torrance, one of the things we've come to expect from the Toros over the last few years is a perfectly executed and highly original routine. Can we expect the same this year?"

Gulp. My stomach did a back flip, thinking about the routines we'd won with in past years.

All courtesy of the Clovers. What could I say? I covered with the kind of double-talk athletes always give the press. "Well, I think every squad goes out there the same way," I babbled, "being as prepared as they can be and just hoping for the best."

She nodded sagely. "I'm sure there's an awful lot of pressure on you, this being your first year as head cheerleader."

It wasn't easy to maintain my smile. "Well, you try not to think about it so much. It's really about the team, and we've been working very hard." Blah, blah, blah. I could hardly believe the stuff that was coming out of my mouth. "We're just glad to be here and eager to see what some of the other squads have come up with."

Out in the arena, the announcer's voice boomed. "And now, the Mighty Muskrats of Mesa Cucamonga!"

And then music filled the air.

Music I'd heard approximately eighty-nine gazillion times in the last couple of weeks. It was the song Sparky had set our routine to.

I turned to look at my squad. They looked as shocked as I did.

"Thank you, Rancho Carne Toros, and good luck!" the reporter finished up.

"Right, thanks," I said, totally distracted. We all nodded politely and backed away from her. Then, as one, we raced toward the stage area.

From the wings, we watched as the Mesa Cucamonga squad struck the exact same lame pose Sparky had taught us. Then, as the music swelled louder and louder, they went into their moves.

Our moves.

The routines were identical.

"Spirit fingers . . ." Missy said, in shock.

Kasey looked outraged. "They stole our routine!"

We all looked at her, rolling our eyes. Someday somebody better give that girl a clue.

I looked back at the Mesa Cucamonga squad. Then I looked out at the audience, as if for inspiration. I had no idea what to do next.

Then I saw a familiar face in the stands. Aaron!

And another. Cliff.

Sitting right behind Aaron. Of course, he didn't know that. He didn't know Aaron. And Aaron didn't know him.

They both happened to spot me at the same time. They both waved.

I waved back.

They both smiled. Then Aaron blew me a kiss, for good luck.

I blew one back to him.

Aaron smiled.

Cliff smiled, too. Hugely.

Oh, my god. I'd just blown a kiss to Cliff!

CHAPTER 23

My face must have been red enough to stop traffic. I stepped back behind the curtain. Still backstage, I watched the Mesa Cucamonga squad for another second. Then I had to stop. It was torture! I grabbed Missy and pulled her deeper backstage. "It's the curse!" I told her.

"What?"

How could she not know what I was talking about? "The Spirit Stick curse," I explained impatiently. Hadn't I just told her that whole story?

Missy stared at me. "Will you lay off with that? There's no curse."

"News flash!" I screeched. "Look around!"

Just then, I heard the announcement I'd been dreading. "Rancho Carne! You're up next!"

Quickly, I rounded up the others. We did a quick huddle, ending with a "SPIRIT!" yell, and took to the stage. We were just going to have to go ahead with our routine. What else could we do? I'd told everyone to smile as big as they could, to jump high and yell loud and stick their positions. With luck, we'd at least be able to make the routine look slightly less pointless than the Mesa Cucamonga squad had.

We struck our opening pose as the music started up. Then we went into our moves. The audience was totally quiet. They must have thought they were seeing an instant replay! I sneaked a peek at the judges and saw them shaking their heads. I couldn't blame them.

As the routine went on, I kept trying my hardest to keep a brave face on things, but there was no denying the humiliation I felt. We went through the moves as if on automatic pilot. I have to give my squad credit; they did their best. The cheesy music blasted away and we smiled our hardest. I felt as if I were in one of those nightmares where you can't find your way out of a horrible situation. The routine felt like it lasted for about five hours.

Finally, we hit our final positions and the music ended. We held the pose for a second. This is the moment when we usually hear tumultuous applause, plus whistling and stomping, from the audience.

This time, there was total silence.

Except for the sound of an empty soda can hitting the floor and rolling down the sloped aisle.

I wanted to die.

The judges sat stonefaced and silent. The audience looked as if they were in shock.

Then I heard something. The sound of one person clapping, slowly and deliberately. It echoed through the arena. I looked up at the audience, scanning their faces until I came to one that was familiar.

It was Cliff.

He was applauding.

CHAPTER 24

My eyes filled with tears as Cliff kept clapping. He began to pick up speed and volume, until, finally, some other audience members began to join in. It wasn't the ovation we were used to, but it was something. I felt like sobbing, but I managed to race off the stage, with my squad behind me.

Who did I run into the second we hit the backstage area?

Isis.

Isis and the rest of the Clovers were standing there, grinning. "That was . . . interesting," said Isis. "Y'all shoulda stuck with our routines." She turned to walk away, and her squad moved to follow her. "We'll send you a postcard from Nationals," she called over her shoulder.

That was the final blow.

Or so I thought. The final blow was yet to come. As I headed for the locker room, an important-looking dude in suit and tie stopped me. He was carrying a clipboard, and I could see by the name tag he wore that he was a UCA official. "Torrance Shipman?"

"Yes?" I had a feeling I knew what was coming, and I didn't like it one bit.

"Tad Freeman," he said, introducing himself. "Universal Cheer Association. We have a problem."

Out of the corner of my eye, I saw Cliff approaching. Truth? I felt like running into his arms. But the timing couldn't have been worse. Missy cut him off at the pass, and I saw them talking. I could just imagine how uncomfortable it was for Missy to have to face her brother after our embarrassing performance. I saw him arguing with her, and he even called out my name at one point, but I couldn't do much to respond.

Tad Freeman continued. "Obviously," he pointed out, "your Toros are not the only squad with this particular routine."

Like, duh.

He peered into my eyes. "Does the name Sparky Polastri mean anything to you?"

Busted. "Sparky Polastri?"

Tad nodded. "Apparently, he's been peddling the same routine up and down the California coast. Six squads total. We're thinking of holding an emergency session of the discretionary panel," he added, in this pompous tone.

"About what?" I was all innocence and naïveté.

Tad looked a little disconcerted. "We've never had a situation like this before. We really should disqualify you."

I didn't stop to think before I spoke. "No!" I cried. "Please don't punish the squad. It was my choice to hire Sparky, not theirs. Don't penalize everyone for my bad judgment." Wow. I don't know where that Mother Teresa routine came from. But, amazingly, it seemed to work.

Tad thought for a second, then held up a hand. "But, since there is no precedent for this, there is nothing in the rule books that forbids it. It's simply frowned upon, and I suppose we can't disqualify you on those grounds alone." He fixed his gaze on me. "Just know that we'll be keeping an eye on you." He made a little notation on his clipboard as if to remind himself to watch those cheatin' Toros. Then he tucked it under his arm. "And don't expect to show up at Nationals with that routine."

He didn't even give me a chance to tell him how eternally grateful I would be for his mercy. He just turned and marched away, all serious and official.

I was left feeling pretty shaky. Then — perfect timing — Big Red and Aaron showed up.

"What are you doing?" shrieked Big Red. (She's so subtle.) "You're wrecking everything I built!"

I couldn't answer. I was on the verge of tears.

Aaron jumped to my defense, sort of. "It's not

totally her fault. I was the one who hooked her up with Sparky —"

Big Red wasn't listening. "This season should've been gravy," she ranted, hands on hips and attitude practically scorching the air around her. "I handpicked the squad. And I delivered an idiot-proof routine." She made a motion like someone putting something on a tray. "Platter," she said flatly. "Nationals. Hello?"

I couldn't let that go by. "Don't you mean 'stolen' routine?" I asked.

Big Red didn't like being challenged. I could have sworn that her curls began to writhe, as if they were snakes. "Don't be naive, Torrance. The truth is that I was a real leader, that I did what I had to do to win at Nationals, and that ever since I handed the reins over to you, you've run my squad straight into the ground."

Ouch. I started to tear up again.

"Spare me." Big Red had noticed how upset I was. And she didn't care. "If I made any mistake as squad leader, it wasn't 'borrowing' routines. It was announcing you as my successor."

That did it. I couldn't hold my tears in any longer, and there was no way I wanted Big Red and Aaron to see me cry. I turned and took off, running blindly toward the nearest exit.

CHAPTER 25

"**T**or! Wait up!" I glanced back to see Aaron pushing his way through the crowd.

I kept moving, but Aaron caught me just before I made it to the door. He grabbed my arm and stopped me in my tracks. I just stood there, looking at the floor. "Let me go!" I said. "I just want to get out of here."

"Wait," he said soothingly. "Big Red's just being a — you know. We all know she can be that way. Even *she* knows it."

I couldn't care less about Big Red. At that point, I just wanted to run away from everything. Maybe she'd been right about me running the squad into the ground. Maybe I couldn't handle being captain. I had no idea what I was going to tell the squad, no idea what direction to go from here. We had a big problem on our hands, and I didn't have the solution. "I don't know what to do here, Aaron!" I wailed.

He held my shoulders and gave me his gentlest smile. "Look," he said, "I know I haven't always been there for you since I went to college. It's been a rough transition — for both of us. But I still care about you as much as I ever did. You know that, right?"

I met his eyes. "You do?" I asked, with a little sniffle.

"Of course. Which is why I hate to see you like this. All stressed out. It's not good for you."

He got *that* right. I softened a little and leaned into him. Aaron can be so comforting. I'd almost forgotten.

"You're a great cheerleader, Tor," he went on. "And you're cute as hell."

I smiled up at him.

"It's just that, maybe —" He seemed to be choosing his words carefully now. "Maybe you're just not exactly captain material. And there's nothing wrong with that."

Huh? Was he really saying what I thought he was saying?

"It's just that . . . maybe you should consider letting Courtney and Whitney take over the squad. They're just like Big Red."

I felt myself stiffen. "You want me to give up captain?" I couldn't believe my ears.

Aaron nodded. "Let them deal with the 'politics,'" he urged. "You just do what you do best. Cheer. I just want to see you happy again. He held me in his arms and stroked my hair. I let him, but I'm not sure why. I did not like what I was hearing. I didn't like it at all.

Aaron talked me into letting him drive me home. It felt so familiar, yet so strange, to sit in the front seat of his Tracker. And to let him kiss me, when he'd pulled up into my driveway.

"Sleep tight, sweetie," he murmured into my ear.

I pulled away. He had no idea how badly his lack of confidence in me hurt. If my own boyfriend didn't believe in me, who did?

I grabbed my gym bag and jumped out of the Tracker. Aaron drove off, and I watched him go. Then I turned and walked toward the front door.

"Friend of yours?" Cliff was standing there, holding a huge bunch of flowers.

I felt as if I'd been punched in the stomach. I didn't need any more surprises that day. And the look of hurt in Cliff's eyes — he must have seen me kissing Aaron — mirrored the hurt I was feeling. It was all too much to deal with. "He's my boyfriend," I said. But was he? "But Cliff, I can explain . . ."

What? What was I going to explain, exactly? I was so confused.

"No, that's cool," Cliff said. "Here." He shoved the flowers at me. "I made you a tape, too." He pushed past me and headed down the driveway.

"Cliff —" I watched him go, and suddenly I

couldn't hold back my tears any longer. I stood there sobbing, wishing he would turn to look back at me.

He didn't.

My day was just about complete.

CHAPTER 26

U ntil my mother started in on me, that is. I'm not sure how she heard about it (no doubt Justin ratted me out), but she did. She cornered me in my room, where I'd shut myself in for a good long cry.

"You hired a choreographer?" She was steaming. "Stealing compounded by *hired* stealing?" She shook her head, giving me that "I'm disappointed in you" look. "You usually have an accurate internal compass."

Whatever *that* meant. "Aaron is right," I said dully. "I should let Courtney and Whitney take over. They have the right personality for it."

"Aaron?" My mother looked at me in disbelief. "Aaron is a moron!"

Jeez, Mom, don't sugarcoat it.

She gave me a closer look. "This isn't like you," she went on. "You're not a quitter."

"I'm not perfect!" I felt like I was letting everybody down, including her. First she didn't even like me to cheer. She wasn't impressed when I made captain. Now she was making me feel bad for wanting to quit. "I want to win," I tried to explain. "I like winning. Maybe I'm just a cheerleader, and not a *leader*-leader. Could you deal with that?"

By then, my dad had joined us. "Winning is great," he said, doing the wise-father thing, "but battling through adversity, winning on a level playing field, being fair . . . well, that's what they write books about, isn't it?" He looked at me gravely. "Let your heart tell you what to do."

With that, the 'rents exited, stage right.

Leaving me to stare at the flowers Cliff had given me. Suddenly, I noticed a chunky white envelope tied to the stems. I undid the ribbon and opened the envelope, and a cassette fell out. I looked down at it, then, figuring I had nothing to lose, stuck it into my boom box.

Oh, my god. Cliff's voice filled the air. He was doing a bad Elvis imitation — or maybe a *good* Elvis imitation. Whatever, it was gooey and sappy and fully demented. "Torrance, Torrance," he sang over a slow guitar riff. I didn't know what to think. This was embarrassing — for me, for Cliff, for anyone who might get their hands on the tape. Still, I couldn't stop listening.

Then, suddenly, the sound changed. Cliff went into an explosive punk riff and started hollering this hard-core anthem.

All about me.

All about how wonderful I am, how beautiful, how talented, how perfect.

I had to laugh. The song was loud and funny and so totally Cliff.

And I was totally into it.

Finally, it ended. I pushed eject and pulled the tape out. Then I just sat there, holding it and thinking.

CHAPTER 27

They waved from across the quad. It was the next day, and the first time I'd seen Courtney and Whitney since the Regionals disaster. I'm not sure what I expected, but leave it to those two to surprise me. When we met up, they threw their arms over my shoulders and squeezed. They were all hearts and flowers, hugs and sympathy.

Hmm. Something told me to be on the alert.

Sure enough, Courtney got right down to it. "Aaron called us last night. He told us you're turning the squad over to us."

I looked at her, raising an eyebrow. I didn't say a word.

Whitney chimed in. "We want you to know that just because you bit the big one as captain, that does not mean we're going to be superhard on you."

Courtney held up a hand as if taking a vow. "We will treat you as if you did not totally mess up any chances we ever had of being a winning squad."

"Gee, thanks." How could I ever repay them?

By then, the rest of the squad had joined us. Courtney and Whitney took up power positions in front of them. "Torrance is not to be harmed!" Whitney ordered.

I saw a few eyes rolling. Courtney went on with it. "We have already decided on a course of action," she informed the squad. "We're gonna forgo Nationals this year."

Whoa! I looked around at the squad. Not one of my teammates would make eye contact with me.

"Everybody's already agreed to it," Whitney told me.

Then Missy spoke up. "Except me."

Leslie shouldered forward. "And me."

Courtney glared at them. "And both of you can be replaced," she said icily.

I was stunned. "I can't believe this."

Courtney shrugged, as if it were no big deal. "Why go to Orlando if we can't win?" she asked.

Whitney nodded ferociously. "East Compton can't say they beat us if we don't show up."

Little Miss Logical Thinking was on a roll.

"So we pull a Michael Jordan," she went on. "Spread the word that after five straight championships, we've gotten bored with Nationals. Say we want to focus on our own community."

I stared at her. Had she gone totally insane? Then I checked the rest of the squad. They were nodding. How could this be happening? This was outrageous.

"Enough!" I cried.

I must have made an impression. I felt all eyes on me.

"Are you people even listening to yourselves?"

Missy gave me a little smile. Courtney and Whitney shot me looks that could have stopped an elephant in its tracks.

"Do not pay attention to her!" Whitney sounded just short of hysterical.

"The queen is dead," decreed Courtney. "Long live the queens!"

I held up a hand. "The only person," I said, speaking slowly and calmly, "who can officially resign the post of captain is the captain." I turned to face Courtney and Whitney. "And I'm not going anywhere."

They looked infuriated. "Then we will have to overthrow you," Whitney choked out.

"Which we will." Courtney was nodding to herself. "You have lost the support of your troops. You are the lamest of the lame ducks."

Was this mutiny? Suddenly, I didn't care what anybody thought. It was time to speak my mind. "Lame?" I asked. "Look at you. It's like I don't even recognize you people." I shook my head in disgust. "I have always thought that we get a bad rap just because we're cheerleaders. That small-minded people see us as dumb and spoiled and shallow. That they judge us for what we do and not who we are. But you know what I just realized? They're all right! We're awful. We're worse than they think. Our whole cheering career, we've staked our reputation on being original, on being the best, the most inventive. Now we finally have a chance to truly be original, and you're all running scared!"

I took a deep breath. I needed one, after that rant.

"She's crazy!" insisted Courtney, taking advantage of the pause.

Whitney gestured wildly. "Someone call a shrink! Stat!"

"I'm not crazy." I stood my ground. "And I'm not resigning as captain, either. You'll have to kill me first!"

"That can be arranged," Whitney muttered.

For a second, there was total silence. Then Kasey — of all people — spoke up. "Shut it, Whitney," she said. "Let her talk."

Courtney and Whitney took a step back, looking shocked. Their mutiny was backfiring.

"I'm not saying it's gonna be easy," I went on, seizing the moment. "But this is an opportunity to show what we're made of! An opportunity to silence our critics!" Were they with me? I wasn't sure yet. But they were listening. "It's gonna be hard work. We'll need a new routine, something amazing and fresh and . . . and . . . storybook. And we've got less than three weeks till Nationals. But if we can do it, if we can pull this off, we prove the skeptics wrong."

They were with me. I felt it. There was, like, this jolt that went through the group. It was time to tie it up. "You say we're losers? I say we've got nothing to lose!"

"Yeah!" Missy pumped her fist.

"You go, girl." Leslie grinned at me.

Kasey was nodding, and I saw a smile on Darcy's face.

"Now, who's with me?" I asked.

"I am!" Missy was the first to jump forward.

"Yeah, definitely." That was Leslie.

Then Jan broke into a smile. "Sounds okay to me," he said.

That was all it took. Suddenly, they were all mine again. All except Courtney and Whitney, that is. They just stood there, pouting like kids who'd made a bad Pokémon trade. I forced myself to smile at them. Like it or not, we needed their help if we were going to do this. "How about it, girls?" I asked. "It's gonna be hard without you two."

They looked at each other. I think they knew they'd blown it.

"Fine," Courtney conceded.

"Whatever," Whitney agreed.

I smiled. "Okay, let's do this."

CHAPTER 28

And so it began.

But what about that new routine? Where was it going to come from? I had a few ideas. But I was also totally freaked. After all, I'd never invented any kind of routine before. So I called the whole group together for a major brainstorming session. After a few hours of intensive discussion, we came up with a plan. We all agreed our best chance would be to draw from a whole bunch of different movement styles. After all, cheering can get stale. Everybody was doing the same old stuff. It was time to bring in some new blood. The question was, where to start?

First, Leslie, Missy, and I went over my entire cheerleading archives, going through each tape in slow-mo, freeze-frame, fast-forward, reverse, whatever it took, to check out every single move we might possibly want to incorporate.

Next, I got in touch with this couple who'd managed to teach my parents (each of whom has at least two left feet) to swing dance. Paul and

Carol spent an afternoon showing us the slickest, hippest moves, all lindy hop and jitterbug. Throws, spins, twirls, and jumps like nothing I'd ever seen before.

After that, it was time for something a little more spiritual. Master Dave, Justin's Tae Kwon Do *sensei*, showed us some centering techniques (we practiced in his Zen garden), then taught us a series of kicks and flips that blew my mind. And made me prepared to fight off potential muggers to boot.

Mime was next. I can't say any of us enjoyed pretending to be imprisoned behind a glass wall, but at least Monsieur Le May didn't make us wear the white face paint he was sporting. And I'm sure we gained something from the lesson, if only the potential to be really, really obnoxious at street fairs.

And finally, modern dance. Yes, really. The kind where you have no idea what the dancers are trying to convey, but you have to admire the way they're twisting themselves into pretzels. Missy called on a friend from L.A., an intern with a dance troupe. She helped us create this awesome free-form pyramid thing, where Darcy was, like, balancing sideways. ("Look, I'm a flying buttress!" was her exact quote at the time.)

We put it all together, and then we rehearsed. And rehearsed.

And rehearsed.

We were all exhausted and bleary-eyed. I don't think there was one of us without a sprained *something*.

But it felt good. So good.

CHAPTER 29

It felt so good, in fact, that I decided to ride the wave and take care of some unfinished business. I borrowed my dad's car one afternoon and drove up to Cal State. After parking in the visitors' lot, I found my way to Aaron's dorm. A few minutes later, I was knocking on his door.

"Hey, babe!" He looked surprised when he opened the door. "What're you doing here?"

"I'm breaking up with you," I said.

Now he looked beyond surprised. Try stunned.

"And by the way," I informed him as I turned to leave, "I'm still captain." I gave a little cheer as I walked away. I didn't care if Aaron was watching me go or not, but just in case, I flipped my hair and gave my hips an extra twitch.

So much for guys who don't believe in me.

Like, who needs that?

CHAPTER 30

Two days later, it all came crashing down. Jan was spotting me as I bench-pressed eighty pounds in the weight room (yup, I had us all pumping iron as part of our new regimen) when Missy burst in. "East Compton can't go to the Nationals!" she blurted. "A thousand bucks per girl is way more than they can raise in time. They're not going."

I couldn't believe it. "What do you mean they're not going?" I asked. I put the barbell back in its rack and sat up.

"That's great news!" Jan was all smiles.

"They cannot not go!" I knew I was shouting, but I couldn't help it. I grabbed a dumbbell and started doing bicep curls. "That's *not* good news!" I pumped harder, until I thought my arm was going to fall off. "Aaaaarrggghhh!" I yelled. "Unacceptable!" I clanged the barbell back onto the rack and grabbed a heavier one.

Jan stared at me. "Considering our chances are considerably improved if East Compton doesn't show, you'll forgive me if I find your response, um, alarmingly numskullish."

He didn't get it. I spoke slowly, carefully. "Best," I said. "Define best. I define best as competing against the best there is out there, and beating them. Winning against the best possible competitors. Period." I slammed the barbell into the rack and grabbed another. "Competing against a field that does not include the best out there does not hearten me! It frustrates me. We" — I grunted as I eked out three more curls — "must — face — them!"

My squad mates thought I'd gone over the edge. So did my family. At breakfast the next morning, I was still on a tear. Then I got this amazing idea. My dad's firm could sponsor the Clovers. It would be a great public relations move for them. All I had to do was convince him. I talked frantically as he tried to eat his Total. "Don't you see?" I asked, after I'd gone over the whole situation. "If they're not there, people will still think we're stealing!"

Justin was amused. "Look, Mom," he said. "Her head is spinning off into another dimension!"

"Shut up," I told him. Then I turned back to my dad. "It's so unfair. The first inner-city squad to ever get a bid to the Nationals, and they can't afford to go!"

My dad shook his head. "The firm gets hit up all the time, hon. I can't."

"It's not that much money, Mr. Level-Playing-Field. Tell them the deal." Now I was pleading. "Maybe they'll want to help." I was appealing to his better nature — and it worked.

"I'll make the call," he said, wiping his mouth on a napkin as he finished his cereal. "They'll probably say no."

"Don't let them!" I followed him as he went in search of his briefcase. "Think how much it will mean to East Compton. They deserve to go. Be fair, remember?"

He looked at me, and I saw the pride in his eyes. This was the daughter he'd raised so well. I could tell he liked what he was hearing.

I'd made my point.

I knew he'd ask.

Now all I could do was wait.

CHAPTER 31

Daddy came through.

Yes!

After waiting not-so-patiently for three days, I got the word. His firm would sponsor the Clovers!

I drove out to East Compton High School the next afternoon, bearing the check. I was feeling very pleased — but a little nervous, too. I wasn't sure exactly how to approach Isis.

When I quietly pushed open the gym door, I saw her and her squad sitting in a circle at center court, deep in conversation. I wasn't quite ready to announce myself, so I did what anybody else would do. I eavesdropped.

I was curious.

And their conversation was very interesting. Apparently, they were working on fund-raising ideas. And the best one they'd come up with was to write to this TV-talk-show host, Pauletta Patton. Still, it seemed like a major long shot to me.

A girl named LaFred seemed to agree with

me. But Isis and Lava were hot for the idea. Isis was reading back from a yellow legal pad. "Where we come from, 'cheer' is not a word you hear very often. . . ."

Lava nodded hard. "They should call us inspiration leaders instead. . . ."

Jenelope gasped. "Ooh, I like that. It's deep."

Shaking her head, LaFred protested, "I don't understand why we're writing to some talk-show host. It's like beggin' for charity."

"It's not charity," said Isis firmly. "Pauletta Patton is from our neighborhood."

Lava backed her up. "She'll understand why we need the money."

"Tell her we need it to buy doughnuts," cracked LaFred. "Her big butt will understand that!"

Jenelope shot her a nasty look. "You're being counterproductive."

LaFred raised her eyebrows. "Lava, stop teachin' this girl them words. She's gonna choke on one."

"Better I choke you, La*Fred*." Jenelope gave the name a certain emphasis.

LaFred bristled. "I told you not to make fun of my name," she said. "I was named after my dead father."

"Guys, come on," Isis interrupted. "I bet them white girls from Rancho Carne don't fight like this."

Oh, sure. I almost stepped forward to disagree with her, but she went on.

"That's why they were able to rip us off for so long and get away with it."

LaFred nodded. She pointed at the yellow pad. "Maybe we should tell her about the long night sessions we have."

Lava took the pad and started to write furiously.

"There you go," Isis said. "That's the kind of stuff she'll like."

"Yeah, that's good," Lava agreed.

I decided to make my entrance. I let the door close behind me so they'd think I'd just come in. I figured I would ignore the fact that they were trying to raise funds on their own. Getting money from Pauletta was so unlikely. And now they wouldn't have to bother with writing letters. Isis stood up when she saw me coming and left the circle to meet me halfway.

"You guys *have* to go to Nationals," I declared. No need to beat around the bush. I might as well come right out with my reason for being there.

"Did you come down here just to tell me that?" asked Isis, glaring at me in her usual way.

I handed her the check. "Here." I tried to be as casual as possible. "I got my dad's company to sponsor you guys."

Isis looked at the check. Then at me. Then she started to laugh.

That wasn't what I had expected.

"What is this supposed to be?" she asked. "Hush money?"

She didn't understand. "No!" I said.

"Oh, then it's guilt money," she said. "You pay our way in and maybe you sleep better at night, knowing how your whole world was based on a lie. Well, guess what?" She held the check up in front of my face and, slowly and carefully, ripped it in half. "We don't need you."

Ouch. She wasn't totally wrong about my motivation. Guilt *was* a part of it. But not all. "Why do you have to be so mean?" I asked, feeling dangerously close to tears. "I'm just trying to do the right thing here."

I saw something change in Isis's face. For once, it seemed as if she heard me, really heard me. And maybe she understood that I cared. She stepped in a little closer — only this time without the glare. "Listen," she said quietly. "I have to be strong for my team. That's what a captain does. All the ones before me let us get ripped off and did nothing. That's not gonna happen on my watch."

I nodded. I understood. I really did. "Well, I'm a captain, too, you know. And I'm trying to make it right."

She knew I was telling the truth. I could see that in her eyes. "You wanna make it right?" she asked. "Then when you come to Nationals, bring it. Don't slack up because you feel sorry for us. That way when we beat you, we'll know it's because we're better."

I looked into her eyes. Isis was asking me a favor, and it was one I was glad to grant. "I'll bring it. Don't worry."

"I never do."

We looked into each other's eyes for one last moment. Then I walked away.

CHAPTER 32

Countdown: one week to Nationals. I stood in the hall at school, catching squad members as they flew by and handing out permission slips for our trip to Orlando.

Then I spotted him: Cliff. He walked by, just out of my orbit, wearing headphones. It was his way of pretending he was somewhere else, anywhere else but at school.

I had been thinking about him.

A lot.

And I wanted to let him know it.

I tucked the rest of the permission slips into my backpack and raced after him. When I caught up, I pulled his headphones off. Kind of a cute, flirty move, I thought.

He didn't seem to agree. He just stared at me, no expression.

"Can I please talk to you?" I asked.

"Nope." He turned to leave.

I grabbed him. I knew he was still hurt about seeing me kiss Aaron. "I was upset that night," I said, desperate to explain. "Aaron gave me a ride home. It was just a good-night kiss. It meant nothing."

"That's great." Cliff was still expressionless. His tone was flat.

"And I just wanted you to know that . . . I broke up with him." There. Now he knew everything.

"Congratulations." He put his headphones back on and started walking again. I stood there and watched him go.

"He didn't believe in me!" I yelled, not even caring about who else was in the hall or what they might think of me. "You did!"

That meant everything to me.

I wondered if Cliff could even hear me. Then I saw him shrug. "Whatever," he tossed back over his shoulder.

"That's important to me!" I yelled even louder. "You believed in me!" I was over the edge. And I didn't care.

Neither did Cliff, apparently. He didn't seem to care about anything. He just kept on walking.

CHAPTER 33

They did it. They actually did it.

That afternoon, still in a total funk about Cliff, I went home and snapped on the TV.

The Pauletta Patton show was on. Her special guests?

The Clovers.

Pauletta was just introducing Isis when I tuned in. "Y'all," she told her audience, "this is Isis, like 'O Mighty Isis.' I used to love that show."

Isis smiled. She looked self-possessed, not at all nervous. "Pauletta, we just want to say how thankful we are for your help."

Jenelope burst in, so overjoyed she couldn't contain herself. "Pauletta, you my girl!" she cried. "You the bomb, baby!"

"Oh, Pauletta," LaFred joined in the lovefest, "we love you so much! And I just want to tell you we love you the way you are. You don't have to lose a pound."

The audience cracked up. Isis didn't look so amused. She glared at Jenelope and LaFred.

Then she reached behind her seat and pulled something out. "We're making you an honorary Clover for life," she told Pauletta, handing it over.

Pauletta held it up. It was a Clovers jacket that said *P SQUARED* on it. Get it? Pauletta Patton. Two *P*'s. "I am honored," Pauletta said, checking out the jacket. "I'm gonna look *good* in this."

Then she cut to a commercial. I snapped off the TV.

The Clovers would be at Nationals. And they'd made it happen themselves.

You go, O Mighty Isis.

CHAPTER 34

Orlando.

Our motel was, predictably, decorated in Early Tiki (very tacky). The marquee outside read WELCOME CHEERLEADERS, YOU'RE ALL WINNERS.

Right. Except for the losers.

The place was hopping when we arrived. There must have been eight or ten squads staying there, and every square inch of available space was taken as they squeezed in some last-minute practice. Missy and I headed through the main pool area with the rest of the squad behind us. I checked out the competition.

I wasn't threatened.

A couple of guys were practicing stunt routines, without a flyer. Just pretending to toss and catch.

A couple of girls stood side by side, marking motions and counting as they half did their routine.

Other squad members watched from the balconies, no doubt offering brutal commentary on their competition's skills.

Ah, Nationals. There's nothing like it.

"Is your family coming?" I asked Missy, trying to sound casual. "Mine is. I can hardly believe it."

"My parents are. I don't know about Cliff."

At the sound of his name, I felt my stomach drop to my knees. "I totally blew it with Cliff."

Missy waved a hand. "Forget it," she said. "My brother's an idiot."

I begged to differ. "You're his sister," I reminded her. "You don't see him like I do." I tried to imagine talking to some girl who liked Justin, but the concept was just too bizarre.

By the time we'd gotten through the gauntlet of cheerleaders, pep squads, and dancers, and found our way to our room, I'd remembered everything I didn't like about cheerleading: namely, most of the people who participate in it. So I couldn't argue with Missy when she started ragging on them. "I don't know what's worse," she said, unpacking. "The neurotic cheerleaders or the pressure to win. You know, I could make a killing selling a product like 'Diet Prozac.'"

I laughed. "All the fun with three less calories!" Missy was so sharp. I got serious all of a sudden. "Thanks for being here this season, Missy," I said.

Missy looked at me. Then she mimed a tear running down her cheek. "Tear."

"No, I mean it," I insisted. "This would have been awful without your no-nonsense and mildly irritating honesty."

Missy grinned. "You're welcome. You're very irritating, too."

We smiled at each other.

Outside, night had fallen. But some squads couldn't seem to stop. We heard chants coming from the courtyard. Missy stepped out onto the balcony. "Shut up!" she yelled. "If you don't have it yet, you don't have it! Give it up already."

I liked her attitude.

I liked her brother, too.

But that was over. I had to forget about him and focus on Nationals.

CHAPTER 35

"**W**elcome to sunny Orlando, Florida," boomed the announcer's voice, "for the Universal Cheer Association Nationals 2000!"

The crowd, mostly parents and coaches wearing T-shirts that said things like, *Cheering is contagious, catch it,* erupted into cheers. The TV cameras rolled around on dollies, jockeying for the best shots. A panel of judges was seated front row center, clipboards at the ready. The outdoor amphitheater was buzzing with energy, and multicolored flags from every state flapped in the breeze as the sun shone down on the stage.

Preliminaries had begun.

This was the day the losers would fall away, leaving the best squads to compete the next day, at finals. I was feeling pretty confident. No way were we going to get cut.

"Fifty teams from across the nation have gathered here to compete, but only one squad will walk away with the title of UCA National

Champions 2000. It all begins in just a few moments. . . ."

I was backstage, stretching. So were about fifty-dozen other cheerleaders, in every style and color of uniform you can imagine. The collective anxiety in that area could have powered a decent-sized city. Some squads were praying as they stretched. Others were just concentrating hard. Like the Clovers.

Isis looked fierce.

That was better than scared.

I approached her, a little tentatively. Pulling her aside, I said in a low voice, "Watch going out of bounds. They deduct like crazy for that stuff."

Isis stared at me. "You going for sainthood or something?"

I ignored her. "You don't wanna blow it on something tiny."

"Look." She folded her arms. "My girls and I made it to the big show without your help. We can handle it."

Then she surprised me.

Turning to her squad, she barked out, "Stay in bounds! Anyone steps outside that ugly blue carpet is dead!" She looked back at me. "Happy?"

I had to smile. "Yes."

Isis nodded. "Tell your girl on the end she's a half second ahead of everyone else on all your turns."

That was Darcy. Isis was right. "Okay, I will." I stood there a moment. "Happy?" I asked.

"Yep," she said, allowing herself to smile. "Remember, bring it."

I nodded and walked off. Isis and I had an understanding. Behind me, I heard Isis yelling to her squad. "Okay, let's do this!"

CHAPTER 36

They did it.

The Clovers made it through preliminaries, no problem. Their routine went off without a hitch.

"The field has been narrowed," the announcer proclaimed at the end of the day. "The advancing squads will move on to tomorrow's finals. The real Cinderella story here, of course, is the Clovers, of East Compton, California. . . ."

They did it.

Oh, and by the way: So did we.

CHAPTER 37

The Clovers were on.

And I mean, they were *on*. I had never seen them so hot. They'd looked totally nervous backstage, but I'd heard Isis give them a pep talk about imagining themselves back in their home gym, and it had seemed to work.

When the announcer introduced them, they ran onstage and laid down flat on their backs. The music started loud and got louder, and they jumped to their feet and slammed into their routine.

They *burned* up that stage. They built and dismantled pyramids, ran stunts nobody had ever imagined before, much less seen, and threw dance moves that were so original, so fresh, the audience was left gasping.

The choreography was pedal-to-the-metal. No pauses, no idling, no filler.

The crowd ate it up.

With a spoon.

The amphitheater was shaking — or maybe that was the earth moving.

I'd never seen anything like it.

Nobody had.

My squad and I watched from the wings. When I looked back at my teammates, I noticed that their faces were drained. They were panicking.

Was I?

Not really. I was too into the Clovers' performance to worry about ours.

I looked out at the audience just as the Clovers were finishing up. That's when I saw him. He was sitting a few rows back from my parents and Justin.

Cliff.

Oh, my god.

He spotted me, too. He gave me a little wave. Yesss!

CHAPTER 38

Cliff was there! He'd come to see me perform at Nationals. Well, maybe he'd come to see Missy, too. But he was there. That was the important thing.

Knowing Cliff was in the audience was all I needed to get totally psyched, totally stoked.

As the Clovers ran off the stage, I turned to my squad. "Okay, Toros, let's just go out there and give it our best." I held out a hand. "Hands in."

We huddled, and everybody stacked their hands.

"Trust on three!" Leslie called out. "One, two, three . . ."

"TRUST!" we all yelled.

Just then, the announcer introduced us. We ran out and took up our beginning positions, backs to the audience, heads down.

The music started.

So did we.

It all came together, all the work we'd done

over the last few weeks. The swing classes, the Tae Kwon Do, the modern dance, the weights — even the mime. We blasted through our routine, and I could tell from the audience reaction that they were getting it. They laughed, they gasped, they applauded at all the right moments.

They were into us.

And we were into performing.

We got into that place where everything just flows. No thoughts, no feelings, just physical perfection and absolute synchronicity.

We were awesome.

We nailed our final position, with me locking my stunt. I was at the top and sticking it.

The audience went ballistic.

Had the Toros just won their sixth national championship?

CHAPTER 39

Two hours later, we were standing in the winner's circle. All the other finalists had been eliminated, and it was down to just five squads. We'd made the cut, but we were all incredibly nervous. Especially me. It's all part of being captain. I'd never had the jitters this bad before — but then again, I'd never worked this hard before, and I'd never choreographed an original routine before, either.

Everybody was crying. That's what cheerleaders do, you know. They cry. They cry when they win, they cry when they lose, they cry when they don't know what else to do.

The emcee moved onto the stage, trailing a microphone cord. The moment of truth had arrived. I could feel my stomach doing somersaults. I was getting more and more anxious with each passing second.

"In third place, from New Pope High School in New Pope, Mississippi, the New Pope Cavaliers!" the emcee announced.

A group of cheerleaders stepped forward, still crying. Third wasn't bad, but it wasn't best. My stomach did a back flip.

"In second place," the emcee boomed, "from San Diego California, the Rancho Carne Toros!"

Everything happened at once. Leslie let out a loud whoop. Courtney and Whitney looked ecstatic. Darcy was grinning as she collected the huge trophy an assistant handed over. Then they all gathered around, hugging me and high-fiving one another.

I was in shock.

"You guys aren't mad that we didn't get first?" I asked.

Kasey answered for all of them. "Without you, Tor, we wouldn't even be here."

Wow.

But the emcee wasn't finished. "And now, the winners of this year's National High School Cheerleading Championships. The East Compton Clovers, from East Compton, California!"

"Whooooo!" Jenelope was on her feet, waving her arms. The whole squad was freaking out, jumping up and down and screaming. LaFred and another girl hoisted Isis and Lava onto their shoulders, and they lifted the trophy — a full foot bigger than ours — over their heads.

Go, Clovers.

I couldn't have been happier for them.

CHAPTER 40

When she got down off her squad mates' shoulders, Isis walked over to me, hauling along the huge check that'd been hanging from the back wall. Twenty thousand dollars. That's not chump change.

"Wow, nice check," I told her.

"I just wanted to tell you, captain to captain, that I respect what you did. You guys were fantastic out there."

Wow. A sincere Isis was intense stuff.

"Thanks." I smiled. "You guys were more fantastic."

She stuck out a hand and I shook it. It felt great.

As the Clovers went off to do their mandatory interviews, Missy approached me. She was holding the Toros Spirit Stick. "So," she said, "you think the curse is broken?"

"I don't believe in curses anymore," I told her.

"Oh, really?" She gave me a devilish look, held

out the stick, and dropped it. I let out a little scream, I couldn't help it. We stared at each other.

Finally, I started to laugh. "Well, maybe we should just bury or burn that," I said. "Just in case."

We stood there smiling at each other. Then Cliff pushed his way through the crowds. He walked right up to me.

"So," he said. "Second place. How does it feel?"

I looked into his eyes. "Feels like first," I said.

And then we kissed.

EPILOGUE

So, you're probably wondering what happened next. Like, did I get into college? And did Cliff and I stay together? And what happened to Isis?

I'll fill you in.

I got into Berkeley. (My parents are way beyond thrilled.)

Cliff is here, too. He's my lab partner. And more.

Missy stuck with cheerleading. She's the new captain of the Rancho Carne Toros.

Isis? She's at Berkeley, too. She and I are competing for the title of captain of the cheering squad. She told me to bring it.

I'm going to.